Women are Different

ABOUT THE AUTHOR

Flora Nwapa is Nigeria's first woman novelist, author of the highly praised *Efuru, Idu, This is Lagos and Other Stories, Never Again, Wives at War* and *One is Enough.*

FLORA NWAPA

WOMEN ARE DIFFERENT

Africa World Press, Inc.

P.O. Box 1892
Trenton, New Jersey 08607

Africa World Press, Inc.
P.O. Box 1892
Trenton, New Jersey 08607

First published in Nigeria by TANA PRESS, 1986

First Africa World Press edition 1992

Cover design and illustration: Ife Designs

ISBN: 0-86543-325-9 Cloth
        0-86543-326-7 Paper

CONTENTS

For women . . . who are different

Chapter 1

They came to the school on the same day, having passed the competitive entrance examination to enter the first secondary school for girls set up by the Anglican Mission in Nigeria. Hitherto there was Denis Memorial Grammar School; Orika Grammar School, and far away in Efik land, Hope Waddel.

They sat for the examination in Port Harcourt, and all three of them sat side by side. They did not actually spy on one another, but they were all well disposed to each other.

After the first paper which was arithmetic, Rose wept uncontrollably. Agnes and Dora sympathised with her. They asked her to wipe away her tears, and assured her that she was going to pass her examination. It was Agnes who said that her weeping was a good sign, and dared anybody to bet with her that Rose would pass. Then Dora said that as a matter of fact, they were all going to pass the examination with full marks and that they would all be admitted to the school in January of 1945, and that they would all be in one dormitory.

Rose was cheered by this but she was still sceptical, and as she was about to moan again, over her errors and omissions, Dora took her by the shoulders and shook her so violently that it hurt. 'Look, forget arithmetic and think of English which we will go in for in a few minutes. You can never retrieve your exam paper again, so forget it and . . .' The bell rang.

It was time for the English paper and the three girls walked to the examination hall. Agnes and Dora were quite

1

confident, but not Rose who sat dejectedly in her seat and waited for the paper to be brought by the beautiful white woman, bespectacled, short, wearing a lovely blue dress, a handkerchief tucked neatly into her blue belt.

When she spoke, Rose did not understand a word of what she said. She glanced at the other girls, and felt better, because they too like her showed they did not understand. 'She is speaking through her nose,' Dora whispered to Agnes. Agnes put her finger on her lips which meant that Agnes should keep quiet so that they would understand.

The small white woman must have been conversant in psychology. She stopped, and asked slowly, yet softly, 'Can you hear me?' A group of girls seated to the right of the hall said they could hear her. One of the girls put up her hand, and the white woman asked her to speak. 'We can hear you, but we cannot understand you.' The girls shifted in their seats. Rose was again almost in tears. What was the difference between hearing and understanding? As she thought this over, another girl's hand was up, and the white woman again asked her to speak. 'De people wey no hear you ma, na bush dem commot. We na township girls, we hear you well, but . . .'

The white woman could not hide her amusement. She was already used to pidgin English spoken in the Port Harcourt area. And in the school, there was a rule that forbade girls from speaking pidgin English. She had made a mistake. She should have taken one of her Nigerian teachers with her. So she tried again, speaking more slowly and emphasising words she would not have normally emphasised, and as she spoke, she distributed the examination papers to the girls.

There were about a hundred girls in the hall, and in a short time, she had given them all papers, and then asked them to read the instructions very carefully before they started answering the questions. When she made sure they now understood her, she asked them to start.

Agnes, Rose and Dora wrote away furiously. Rose was in her element. That was her subject. She wrote the essay, read

2

it over and was satisfied. Then she did the comprehension. The grammar was a bit tricky. She tackled that vigorously and earnestly, and when she finished, she heaved a sigh of relief, and looked around. Agnes and Dora were still writing, and so were the other girls in the hall. So Rose turned to her answer paper and began to read her answers all over again. 'You now have ten minutes,' the small white woman said. There was mild commotion. The girls began to tie their answer papers together, and to stretch and yawn.

Time was up and the answer papers were collected by the small white woman. Agnes, Rose and Dora exchanged addresses and went back to their different schools.

What luck therefore for the three of them to meet at the railway station in January of 1945! They had all passed the entrance examination to Archdeacon Crowther Memorial Girls' School (ACMGS) Elelenwa, and they were now going to the school to start their first year. 'Isn't it wonderful that the three of us passed the examinations,' said Agnes. 'And didn't I tell you that you were crying for nothing, that day, Rose,' said Dora.

'I still believe I messed up in that Arithmetic paper. I am sure that's what decided my case, what passed me was the English paper,' said Rose.

'You never can tell' said Dora. 'However,' she continued, 'we three are here, we passed. Thank God.'

So the 'three musketeers' (as they chose to refer to themselves) became great friends. When they arrived at the Umukoroshe railway station they alighted from the train, and they helped one another to put their boxes down.

There were so many girls on the platform. Agnes could recognise three or four faces she saw at the examination hall the year before, and in particular the self-styled township girl who said she understood what the English lady said and referred to the others who did not understand, as *bush*. 'We are going to deal with her,' Agnes and Dora said. 'I don't agree with you,' said Rose. 'The best way to treat such people is to ignore them. The best answer for a fool is silence,' she concluded.

'Whether the best answer for a fool is silence or not, if she insults me, I am going to deal with her. Who does she think she is?'

As she spoke, the girl they were talking about came straight to them, and said, 'I know you, not you three I see for Port Harcourt last year when we do the exam? So una pass too? Me I pass too. But my friend no pass, im fail. And im papa send am go Enitona High School. Imagine, Enitona High School! Not to good school. Na bad school. Na so so belle the girls dey carry when dem go Enitona. I sorry for my friend. Ego carry belle too . . .'

The girls were shocked. What a girl! What precocity!

'Una dey wait?' the girl continued. 'Onyeburu no dey here. We go carry our box for head. Look, look the senior girls dey carry dem boxes for head. And make I tell you, de people we live here, dem too make nyanga. Dem no go carry na boxes for una. Look dem dey poor like church mouse.' As she said this and before the girls had time to say anything, she had left them and gone to see to her boxes and other equipment for school.

It was then that Agnes, Rose and Dora looked round to get a glimpse of their surroundings. The railway station was bare and poor. The train that brought them having proceeded on its long and slow journey to the coal city, Enugu, they became aware of their surroundings. There was just a single railway line, and the station master's office. Behind the office was a two roomed building that belonged to the station master, where he lived with his wife and nine children. At the office, was a hole where one could push in money to buy one's ticket and adjoining the office, was a kind of hall with an old scale used in weighing loads of produce, being transported by Goods Trains to the far North.

The station itself was littered with sugar cane which was abundant in the area. When the trains made a stop at the station, children came with their long sugar cane stems to the

4

windows of the coaches, begging the passengers to buy. When they bought them, the children cut them in tiny lengths for the passengers.

Agnes was tempted to buy, but Dora and Rose dissuaded her, 'Where are you going to keep it?' they asked her. 'I'll eat it, not keep it,' she replied. 'And thus dirty your beautiful dress,' they said. But then the township girl who had spoken to them had already bought ten lengths of sugar cane, and the child she bought them from was busy cutting them into tiny lengths. Agnes could not resist the sugar-cane so she went over and asked how she was going to carry them to the school. 'For head,' she said, chewing one of the sugar cane.

Agnes smiled, 'Well I want to buy some.'

You wan buy? Make I call dem for you.' She turned and hailed another child who came running with about five lengths of sugar cane. Agnes bought some, thanked the girl, and then introduced herself. 'I am Agnes, what is your name?'

'Comfort,' the township girl replied, and Agnes went over to Dora and Rose, and they tried to organise themselves for the long trek to the school.

Agnes and Dora carried what they were able to carry, while Rose and Comfort waited at the station. 'What a pity this school does not have a vehicle,' said Rose. 'Na suffer dem go suffer we for dis school. Mission, dem poor. I know now why I no go Queen's College. I pass de entrance but my Papa say I no go go Lagos. E say im people wey go Lagos never return. Den my Mama say, "to go Lagos no hard, na return".'

Rose roared with laughter. She had never heard that expression before. She said truthfully that she did not take the entrance to Queen's College at all. And that she was prepared to read elementary six, if she failed to gain admission to ACMGS, and try again. But thank God she passed the entrance.

'You see dat big girl wey wear that fine dress?' asked Comfort. Rose of course did not take any notice of the big girl that wore 'a fine dress'. There were so many big girls who

5

wore beautiful dresses whom she took to be their teachers. 'De one wey wear yellow dress. Wey make im hair. Na de prefect. Dem say ibi good prefect. De teachers like am too much. But e too old. Dem say e done reach twenty years. But im look small, like ibi small pikin. But ino bi small pikin o! Dem dey call am Oby.' As she said this, she laughed again. 'OBY. What is OBY?' asked Rose. Comfort laughed again, and said, 'I no go tell you. Ibi big secret. If de girl I know say you know, igo punish you well well. But I go tell you. You bi my friend. OBY is "old but young".' Rose roared with laughter, and as she was laughing the other children returned to carry their other belongings, and as they were walking slowly to the school, there was the sound of the train. The girls crossed the railway line quickly and made their way to the school, while the train, this time coming from Aba, was bringing the girls resident in Aba and its environ to ACMGS.

Comfort seemed to know everything about the school, and told the girls one story after another. She told them that the teachers were very strict and that they were going to confiscate extra dresses from the girls. They were allowed only six cotton dresses, and ten shillings pocket money a term. If they had more than ten shillings, the teachers would take them from them. She told them she brought some cooked food with her though it was against the regulations of the school. But she knew how to hide the food, and she would invite them to eat it after lights out.

What a girl, Rose thought. Agnes and Dora were most intrigued also, and asked questions upon questions. Comfort had all the answers. Nothing was impossible for her. She knew how to wriggle out of any problem.

What a school, Rose thought. The whole place was bush. Both sides of the road was thick bush, there was no clearing of any kind, not even a hut or a farm. Why did she not think of Queen's College, Lagos. If she passed the entrance examination to ACMGS, surely she would have passed that of Queen's College. Both were equally competitive. Why did she not know about it? But then who was around to direct her? Her aunt who could have, was far away in Achimota College, in Ghana. The uncle who could have directed her was in far away Fourabay College Sierra Leone. Her own mother was dead years ago, and her father was so busy with his work that he had no time to think about his daughter's education.

'I don't think I like this school,' Rose said aloud. 'Say that again,' Agnes echoed.

'I like am o. Make I tell you. If you no go Elelenwa, which school you go go – Enitona?' Comfort asked in her usual way.

'What about Queen's College?' Rose asked.

'You no hear? "To go Lagos no hard na return." I done tell you.' Agnes and Dora laughed. Rose joined reluctantly.

'I would have gone to QRC, Onitsha,' said Agnes, 'but my step mother preferred Elelenwa. And I had no choice in the matter. However, I am glad I passed. It is good to be away from home for a change,' she said.

The girls walked on and on until they arrived at the school. There was no gate. There was only a tiny sign board indicating the school from the main road, and as they entered the premises, they saw that the so-called school was surrounded by bush. To their right was a building they called the office. There was an arrow that pointed to the buildings they called the classrooms. In the middle of the building was a large hall. There they entered.

There were two teachers on duty. There were also fresh girls like them. The teachers spoke only English. They asked them to open their boxes, and they examined them and saw that they had the right number of dresses. If they had any money they were to surrender it to the teachers who would make a note of it.

It was strange, very strange. But, all four girls were assigned to the same house, called 'Clock House'. A distant relation of Rose was also in that house. Rose later learnt that it was done on purpose so that her relation would take care of her. But where was this relation, her friends asked her. Rose told them that she lived at Enugu and that the Enugu train would come in the evening. She assured him that her cousin would look after them well.

The girls settled very quickly in their dormitories and then came out to play in the field. They asked for a ball which they were given and they played netball. They were good at the game, except Rose, who did not play very well, but she enjoyed the game all the same.

Soon it was time for lunch and the bell went so they trooped to the dining-room taking their plates, cutlery and cups with them. When some of the girls saw the food in the bowl they began to cry. Comfort cried the most. She had okra and stew, eba and rice alright to eat afterwards, but she cried because she thought that before Sunday, and it was just Friday, the food would finish and she would starve. As for Rose, the food was worse than she had imagined. She had heard that feeding was poor, but not to that extent. At home, she missed her mother who died three years before, but her home was quite orderly, meals were served hot by well trained stewards. Her father, though he had not married again, made sure that she and her brothers and sisters fed well. Feeding well was the priority in her home. And now this. Why, why did she not think of Queen's College where she had learnt only that morning that the girls in that school were waited upon by stewards, had running water, cooks, and what was more, played tennis.

She must have been deceived. But deceived by whom? She must stop that nonsense. Dora and Agnes had told her that the sooner she stopped thinking of Queen's College, Lagos, the better for her. So she made a serious effort to like Elelenwa.

She and her friends ate very little at table. Comfort had told them that she had some food in the dormitory and that she was inviting them all to come and eat. So they trooped to her bedside, and ate to their hearts' content. Comfort had very good quality. She gave generously and never counted

8

the cost. But she also expected you to give generously when she herself was without. So woe betide you if you had food and hid it from Comfort when you had shared her food with her in the past! Rose, Dora and Agnes learnt this very quickly, and though they did not very much want her to move in their circle, because of her 'loud mouth', they made sure that whenever they could, they shared their food with her. But they were more comfortable if she did not invite them to eat with her.

After the meal, the girls trooped to the office to pay their fees to the principal. They queued outside the office waiting for their turns. Rose was the first to go in. She saw the small white woman at close quarters, and observed that she was a pretty woman. Because she was near, she was able to hear and understand her well, though she made some noises, like eh . . . eh. The principal, who before she received Rose's school fees told her that her name was Miss Hill and that she was known to the girls as Miss Hill, was very gentle and kind. Rose was able to observe her well. She wore a pink check dress which was well tailored. She had the white handkerchief over her belt as she did on the day of the entrance examination in Port Harcourt. Her hair was long and clean. There was a kind of scent emanating from her which Rose could not recognise. It was after she had remained in the school for four years that she discovered that Miss Hill used Blue Grass perfume by Elizabeth Arden.

Miss Hill's office was spacious, but bare. The writing desk was just an ordinary wooden table. She did not see a filing cabinet. But there was a shelf containing some books. Miss Hill wrote in a large note book. And Rose observed that when she came in and greeted her, she turned the pages of the note book, and then wrote on a fresh page. When she had paid her fees Miss Hill asked her how much money she had. 'Ten shillings,' she replied.

'I have ten shillings,' Miss Hill said.

'Ten shillings' Rose repeated. Miss Hill smiled and said, 'Rose, you reply with a sentence. When I ask you how much money you have, you don't say ten shillings, you say, "I have ten shillings".' Rose replied, and realised immediately that she was having her first English lesson.

Soon Miss Hill finished with the girls, and again they went out to play netball. As they were playing, they heard the sound of the train, and they realised that the Enugu train had arrived. They stopped playing and ran to the railway station to welcome the girls coming from Enugu. Rose's cousin was one of them. They were in time for the train. And they helped the girls take their belongings down from the train.

At the assembly in the evening, Miss Hill spoke to the girls. The new girls felt better. Agnes, Dora and Rose sat together wondering whether their parents did the right thing by sending them to the school. But in the few days that followed they adjusted to the routine of the school, and discovered that though it was hard, especially getting up at five thirty in the morning to fetch water half a mile away; doing house work, and cooking the meals, they enjoyed their classes, their games, and reading.

They were now exposed to the new world of books. Stories fascinated them, and they read everything they could lay their hands on, including 'True Romances' which Miss Hill or to be more precise, the regulations, forbade them to read. One of the older girls smuggled in the magazine to the school, and girls read them to their hearts' content.

Agnes, Rose and Dora shared books. Comfort went as far as 'stealing' library books from the school library, and reading them during lessons like Maths, which she was not good at. Some senior girls brought in books by Marie Correlli which the girls read with so much zeal, but which were forbidden in the school. The girls wondered why Miss Hill and Miss Backhouse frowned at their reading Marie Corelli. They did not find the answers, for they dared not bring up the topic at all, but they read volumes and volumes of them when they laid hands on them.

What pleasant times the girls had in their school! What good relationship existed between the staff and the girls!

Rose could remember when she first menstruated. Because she had no mother, she was not warned. Then just out of the blue, she found herself bleeding. She was genuinely afraid. What was happening to her? Who was she going to confide in? Not Susy who was older than she and a relation, not her friends, Dora and Agnes. But she went straight to Miss Hill, and knocked at the office door during prep. She knew she was not allowed to leave her classroom during prep, but she felt that it was the only time she could go and not be seen by the other girls. She wanted as much privacy as possible.

'Come in Rose,' Miss Hill called. Rose opened the door quietly and went in. 'I know you should be at prep now, but you must have something important to say. Are your father, brothers and sisters well?'

Rose burst into tears. 'I . . . I . . . am . . .' she choked 'I . . . I am blee . . . ding . . . Miss . . . Hill . . .'

'Sit down child.' She went to the adjoining room, and brought a pad. Take this. Use it. You are menstruating. It is natural. Didn't Susy tell you? She should have warned you. Don't worry child, you are all right. You have reached womanhood. Here, take this,' and she gave her two tablets of aspirin.

As far as Rose was concerned, Miss Hill was talking Greek. It was only when the nuisance occurred again, and from what she read in True Romances, did she know what she was in for. 'Oh God!' she said to Dora one day, 'for the rest of my life, this bleeding occurring every month. God, what a life.'

So Rose, Agnes and Dora got more and more interested in True Romances, and therefore in boys. The senior girls talked about their boy friends a lot. But the 'Three Musketeers' felt they were too young to talk of boys. It was Agnes who, after giving a thought to what was happening to them, (they were all passing from one phase of life to the other) convinced them that they should begin to give boys a thought. If they were eventually going to get married, the sooner they started having boy friends the better.

11

They were discussing this point one night after lights out when Comfort joined them. Comfort in her characteristic way warned them that they were all going to end up 'carrying belle'. They so roared with laughter, that the prefect was awakened and warned them that if they did not stop their nonsense she was going to report all of them to Miss Hill in the morning. They knew that their prefect was a kind and good prefect. She had never reported anybody to the principal or to any of the teachers since she was made a prefect. Nevertheless they did not want to be in trouble with her, so they quietly went to bed.

Well, as luck would have it, there was an announcement the next morning that Okrika Grammar School boys were coming for a debate in the school. The Debating Society had organised this event the year before, but for one reason or the other, it did not get off the ground. Now everything was well in hand and in two weeks, they could come. The girls were excited. The senior girls had nothing else to discuss but the impending visit of their brother school. Those who were to speak had prepared their points with the help of the teachers. The topic was 'That the education of girls is a waste of money'.

Rose thought the topic was silly. Dora and Agnes agreed with her. But Comfort said she believed that their parents were wasting their money educating them. They would eventually marry, have children and forget all they learnt in school. Rose pointed out that she had read somewhere where it was said that the hand that rocked the cradle ruled the world. Comfort said that the hand that rocked the cradle was not necessarily an educated hand. All that mattered to women was getting married and having children and starting a beautiful home. She pointed out that she did not understand why the missionaries should forego marriage. Dora told her that nobody was talking about marriage and spinsterhood. The topic was that the education of girls was a waste of time.

Then Comfort took it from that point, 'Yes, you should take it further by saying, why educate girls then give them in

12

marriage before they are fifteen years of age. Teach them how to sweep the floor, cook, wash and iron clothes, take care of the home generally, be able to knit and sew : . .'

'In short teach them domestic science,' one of the girls put in.

'That is education,' Rose said.

'That is not education the way we know and understand it. What you are talking about is the type of training my mother received before she married my father,' said Comfort. And the girls roared with laughter.

They did not know that one of the senior girls was listening to them, and was quite interested in their argument. So Comfort and Rose were surprised when they were told that Miss Onu wanted to see them at break time. Said Miss Onu, 'I was told about your discussion on the topic for debate. Would you like to speak on the occasion?' The girls expressed the willingness to speak, and when the rest of the school heard it, they were angry. The girls were merely children in form one. The boys from Okrika Grammar School were senior boys, and therefore were not the match of the two girls. How dared Miss Onu suggest such a thing. If care was not taken, the form one girls would be made prefects! But the senior girl who heard the girls' argument was highly impressed. She did what she did in good faith. So to avoid unnecessary trouble, the Junior Debating Society was formed. The Principal of the brother school was informed, and since that school already had a Junior Debating Society, it was quickly agreed that rather than have one event there should be two events involving the two debating societies.

But two days to the day, the kit car which was to drive the boys to ACMGS developed engine trouble. Miss Hill was so upset. She had had so much trouble over the debate, and whatever was in her power to do, she would do to please the girls. There was a staff meeting and there it was decided that the girls could go to Okrika by canoe. Anybody who did not want to go because she was unable to swim, and therefore might be afraid of water could remain behind.

Thank God! Rose could swim. Comfort could not swim, but she said she would go all the same; the canoe was not going to capsize. Agnes and Dora were all swimmers, and assured the others that if anything happened they knew how to save them from drowning. 'But why should we go by water? The boys should take the risk, not us?' objected one of the teachers. 'The trip is dangerous,' she argued. But she was overruled by everyone.

The day came. The girls in the Debating Societies were ready. Their uniforms were well starched and ironed. They had their beautiful scarves on their heads, and wore their sandals. Those who had no sandals borrowed sandals from those who had but were not members of the societies. Miss Onu was looking very smart in her native attire. She was the idol of some of the girls, especially Rose. Rose simply adored her for her beauty, smartness and knowledge. She was next to Miss Hill as far as Rose's thinking was concerned.

Miss Onu was a good looking petite young woman who had just left United Missionary College in Ibadan to teach in ACMGS. She went to Queen's College to crown it all, a school Rose regretted not having the privilege to attend. She taught the girls in form one, English and mathematics, and to Rose's childlike mind, she was, apart from Miss Hill followed perhaps by Miss Backhouse, an ideal teacher. No African teacher had ever taught her the way Miss Onu taught her maths and English.

The girls lined up in twos, and set out for the canoe. The path to the stream was rough and winding. There were trees with fruit which were edible and in season, and the girls wished that Miss Backhouse was with them to pluck the fruit and learn their different parts. They decided however that the next time they had their botany class, they would ask Miss Backhouse to let them visit the bush and fetch plants and insects that inhabited the area.

They were soon at the edge of the water, and the ferrymen were there waiting for them. It was not thirty minutes before they reached Okrika. The boys were waiting for them. At long last, they were there. They were taken round by the boys. Rose, Comfort, Agnes and Dora noticed that not a single junior boy of their age was anywhere near. The boys who came to receive them were big boys in classes four, five and six. What was happening? But the girls waited in apprehension.

Furthermore, the senior girls were not happy at what was happening. It appeared as if the boys were more interested in the younger girls than them. They too waited in anticipation.

Meanwhile the senior prefect of the school had taken Miss Onu to the Principal's house, and the girls were gathered into the hall where the debate was going to take place. While they waited, things began to get out of hand. A senior girl disappeared, followed by a junior one; and before the girls were called for lunch there was no one left in the hall.

Nobody was left alone of course. The boys made sure that everybody had someone beside him. And by the time the debate started, names and addresses had been exchanged.

The climax of the outing was not the debate as much as the entertainment after the debate. The boys sang, and acted and made the girls feel at home. The girls sang and returned their gratitude for a well spent day. Nobody thought about the means of returning back to School. Though of course Miss Onu knew that the girls would be driven back to their school, some fifteen kilometres away.

At long last, since everything that has a beginning must have an end, the day finally was closing. The kit car which was understood to have been repaired in the afternoon was nowhere to be found. Soon it was six, seven, eight o'clock at night, and the girls had to go back to their school. It was too late to go by canoe. The only form of transport available was walking. If the girls were to go back to school that night, they had to walk. And since they could not walk all by themselves, the boys had to walk them to their school, and walk back again.

Was this a coincidence, or was it well thought out and

15

organised? The kit car developed engine trouble before the girls set out; they therefore came by canoe. It was the same kit car that was again to be used to convey the girls back to their school. The school did not have another vehicle. As a matter of fact the school, like ACMGS, owned no vehicle at all. The kit car was hired from Port Harcourt. Neither of the Principals of the schools had a vehicle, though it was whispered that the Principal of Okrika Grammar School had a motor-cycle, or was it a bicycle?

If this was organised it paid dividends to the organisers. The boys of the Grammar School volunteered to walk the girls of Elelenwa back to their school that night. It did not cross anybody's mind to think and suggest that the girls could be quartered that night on the school premises. Miss Hill would never allow the girls to spend a night in a boys' school! And she was right, there was no danger of any kind, and therefore the girls must return.

The boys and girls set out. Many boys had volunteered to do the eighteen to twenty kilometres of walking. The moon was bright, brighter, because there was no electric light to interfere with its natural glow. The stars could be seen quite distinctly. It was Miss Backhouse who taught the girls the names of the stars, and they glowed thousands and thousands of kilometres in the sky. As far as Rose, Comfort, Agnes and Dora were concerned, they could walk to the moon that night. Everybody had a partner to walk her home, and everybody was engrossed in her partner. What the girls read in 'True Romances' were making meaning to them. The record song books, and the words in them sprang into life. The girls sang, the boys sang, they held hands, they kissed. It was heaven.

Some walked very fast to avoid being seen by others, while some lagged behind. Suddenly someone started a song:

'If you were the only boy in the world
And I were the only girl,
Nothing else would matter in this world today

16

We would go on loving in the same way old way
The garden of Eden was just meant for two
With nothing to mar one's joy
If I were the only girl in the world
And you were the only boy.'

As far as the boys and girls were concerned they were, each
pair, Adam and Eve in the Garden of Eden. They were
floating in the garden, enjoying the breeze, the trees, the
birds, the numerous fruits. They were all theirs to eat and
enjoy. They were happy, they were innocent; they had not
yet eaten of the forbidden fruit. So what else mattered in the
world, except holding hands, singing love songs, and
walking from Okrika Grammar School, to ACMGS,
Elelenwa at night, with a full moon? Not a snake dared
disturb the boys and girls, not an insect dared perch on them.
The snakes and insects and all the dangerous animals, if
there were any, all steered clear. Or maybe they watched the
pairs as they walked by, two by two, oblivious of any fear,
any obstacle, any danger.

It was long ago. There were thieves all right, but not
daring ones. The kind of thieves we had were the ones who
came quietly to steal at night making sure you and your
family were asleep. If you were a light sleeper, and woke up,
they got frightened, and ran away, leaving you in peace. If
thieves walked along the road at night, and heard a sound,
they did not confront you. They disappeared into the bush
again, and let you go your own way in peace, then stole out
again and resumed their nocturnal business. Even a mere
child could frighten the most daring of thieves, because he
was unarmed, and therefore had nothing to fight with.

In those days, thieves when caught were not handed over
to the police, especially when they were caught at night, the
head of the household got him, and with a six inch nail,
nailed his fore-head, pushed him out of the compound, in his
home.

Meanwhile the girls who'd stayed at school became

17

restive. They were unable to go to bed. When the first lights out bell rang, they decided to go to Miss Hill to register their fear. They were assured that the girls who went to Okrika were safe and would return. Could they go in search of them? Miss Hill asked them to wait for an hour, and if they did not return then the night watchmen would be asked to go.

It turned out to be the longest one hour the girls had ever spent. They again rushed back to Miss Hill who was sitting in the office. She was already in her nightdress and dressing gown. 'You can go girls, while we wait here,' she said.

So the girls, also in their nightdresses and wrappers, with their hurricane lamps in hand, ran towards the railway station. It was nearly ten o'clock at night. Crossing the railway line, they were tired. Some went back, but the more daring ones went on, not running this time, but walking slowly and steadily.

Both groups coming from the opposite direction were becoming tired. The bliss was giving way to tiredness and even hunger. The girls longed for their beds; and the boys who could no longer walk further, turned back. A junior boy who insisted on walking the girls home, because he felt that one of his prefects would talk to his sister, was so tired, that his friends had to carry him physically back to the school. At one point in the great trek the school prefect announced that all junior boys must return to school, leaving the senior boys to walk the girls home.

It was a wonderful feeling, a wonderful opportunity to be able to stay together a whole day, and part of the night inclusive. When the junior boys went back, the senior boys organised themselves again, and made one more supreme effort to see the girls safely to their school, though the love songs were dying on their lips.

Far off, lights were seen. At first, they appeared like the tiny lights of insects that inhabited the area. But as the boys went further, the tiny lights were getting bigger and bigger.

The girls from ACMGS walked further on, and because the boys of the Grammar School did not have lights, the girls

18

from home did not see them in time. Then, the girls saw them, and charged forward, both hands outstretched and embraced any moving object that was visible. When the boys saw what was happening, they moved forward and were rewarded by more and more embraces from the school girls. What good fortune! What a day well spent!

Thank God their fellow girls had come in search of them. Was it not wonderful to care so much for one's own school mates? The ACMGS girls did not know that the Grammar School boys were seeing the girls home. They had come, out of the goodness of their hearts, in search of their fellow girls.

Now that ACMGS was almost in sight, the thought of trekking back to the school came to the forefront. The boys could have walked another eighteen or twenty kilometres if the girls were walking with them. Now the girls were almost in their school, the boys had to return to their school. They walked on and on, then one of the boys began to sing: 'One more river to cross the Jordan' and everyone joined in. The 'River Jordan' in this case was the railway line. Yet when they reached the railway line, they walked on, until they came to the gate of the school, where Misses Hill and Backhouse, stood, like white ghosts, with their hurricane lamps in their hands.

It was an eloquent sign that the boys were not allowed to go beyond them. Reluctantly the boys said good bye, and one of them started a song, 'Kiss me Goodnight, Sergeant Major'. The girls sang, saying goodbye, leaving the boys, and going into their school.

The boys waited until everybody had gone in. 'The Three Musketeers' including Comfort were the last to enter their compound. Miss Hill took note. She thanked the boys, said goodmorning and goodbye to them, and stood as the boys turned back and took the first steps of their weary journey back to their school, this time without the girls.

Chapter 2

The 'Three Musketeers' as well as Comfort were in trouble.
Miss Hill had made a note when she saw them the morning
the Grammar School boys brought them back to school. She
was shocked to have such precocious girls in her school. She
would have thought that the four girls would be the first set
of girls to return, not the last. She expected that kind of
behaviour from her more senior girls not girls who were in
their first year.

She did not call the girls to her office until the beginning of
the new term. She had wanted to ignore the incident of last
term since the girls were not responsible for the kit car
breaking down again, and if anything had happened to the
girls that night, she and the teachers were to be held
responsible. But of late the four girls had been receiving a
series of letters from boys especially boys from the Grammar
School, and elsewhere.

Miss Hill knew the writing of each girl in the school. The
girls were supposed to post their letters written on Sundays,
in Miss Hill's office. She had not seen letters written by these
girls, yet she had seen many letters addressed to them. What
had happened to the innocent girls during the holidays?

Miss Hill did not know that a lot happened that night. The
four girls had had their first kisses, not from younger boys of
their class, but from senior boys in classes three and four.
They had agreed that they would meet in Port Harcourt
during the holidays. They had actually met, went to see
films, and had quite a good time. Dora had met Chris, and
now was writing to him regularly; Rose was writing to

Ernest, and Agnes was writing to Sam. As for Comfort, because she performed so well at the debate, she was writing to four boys in the same school, and many more in Denis Memorial Grammar School and Hope Wadell. She bragged about it. She said she wanted to have a boy-friend in Kings College, Lagos. Why should the girls of Queen's College, Lagos monopolise the boys of King's? It did not strike her that the Girls of ACMGS were monopolising the boys of the Grammar School. In pursuing this policy, if one could call it so, Comfort got into serious trouble in the boys' schools where she operated. She caused so much confusion and trouble, that in her third year, all the boys who wrote to her, after series of quarrels, got together and decided that she was not worth all that trouble, and therefore abandoned her. But Comfort did not mind. As insensitive as she was she even told the story herself and laughed with the girls. 'What I know is that I am not going to put all my eggs in one basket.' One thing with Comfort was that she spoke the King's English as well as she spoke the pidgin English spoken in Port Harcourt area. To some girls it was not easy.

One of the girls who was not all that flushed about boys was Agnes. She wrote to Sam all right, but not with the zeal of her other friends. Rose was almost fanatical about Ernest. She wrote him every week whether he replied or not. Her friends thought she was stupid and said so to her, but she said she could not help herself. Comfort told her that if she wrote to a boy and he did not reply in a fortnight, she lost interest. A boy, she insisted, must have the responsibility to reply to her letter on time. She hated to be ignored, and ended up by saying that she would never give anybody the chance to ignore her. 'The person, boy or girl, who will ignore me has not been born,' she frequently said.

Agnes was quieter during the second term. Something must have happened to her during the holidays. She had told the girls that she lived with her father and her father's wife. She did not like her, but who did? She did very little and concentrated on her school work. She would not talk much about her home during conversations.

Miss Hill called the girls one after the other and talked to them about their love lives. She told them they spent more time writing love letters, and less time doing their school work. And warned them that if they continued in that way, she was going to report them to their parents.

Comfort made nothing out of it. Dora and Rose were a bit shaken, Agnes was in tears. She went privately to Miss Hill and begged her not to give her a bad report. 'That will be the end of me and my schooling,' she said. Thereafter, Miss Hill sat her down and asked her to confide in her. She did. She was under pressure to get married to someone she did not like. He was much older than herself – no, he was as old as her father, but because her step-mother wanted to get rid of her fast by marrying her off, she had convinced her father that the man was good for her. She loathed the man, but there was nothing she could do on her own. All she was asking of the Principal was not to write an adverse report on her. That would give her father more cause to marry her off during the holidays. She knew her own mind, and she was determined to be in school and take the Cambridge School Certificate examination before she married.

Miss Hill had a thousand and one things to say to the girl, but she did not. After all she thought, she was a foreigner in a foreign land with strange cultures. She was not going to interfere. If she could, or she had the opportunity, she would talk to Agnes' father on her behalf. She would tell Agnes' father that his daughter was brilliant, and it would be in his best interest to give her a full secondary school education, and then marry her off if he must.

What was the use of spending so much time and energy teaching a child algebra and geometry and all the other subjects if she was not going to make use of them? Wasn't that other missionary right in recommending that the school which Miss Hill carefully set up to educate the elite of Nigerian women, should be down-graded, and used for the training of Cathechists, and church agents' wives? She had

22

opposed that other missionary's views so vehemently at the conference when the topic was discussed. Perhaps, in view of what was happening she, Miss Hill was wrong.

But she felt Nigeria needed well brought up Christian girls who would take their places when they eventually handed over power to the people. Miss Hill could see the handwriting on the wall since the advent of Fr. Nnamdi Azikiwe.

To counteract all these bad influences, the missionaries and the colonial government in Nigeria needed schools of the status of ACMGS. They as missionaries should teach these girls properly, and that was exactly what she was doing. But then other influences intervened. Agnes' father would not even allow her to have a four year education. She had not graduated in Oxford and come to Nigeria to train Nigerian girls to be good wives. She was not a wife. She was a missionary who had shunned all worldly attractions to do the will of God.

Newspapers, though scarce in those days were not read in the school. Rose received *The West African Pilot* the other day by post, and Miss Hill had to confiscate it. However when Mbonu Ojike wanted to speak to the girls on the Ibo language, Miss Hill allowed him to come, though she refused the request of Dr. Nwafor Orizu, perhaps because of his bombastic English. (He had, the year before spoken to the boys of the Grammar School, and after his lecture, the Principal thanked him for his entertainment!)

Miss Hill was interested in Mazi Mabonu Ojike because he was keen on the preservation of the Ibo language and culture. The girls were encouraged to sing and dance Ibo dances, and speak Ibo in school (it was pidgin English that she disallowed). Ibo language was one of the subjects taught in school, and church services were conducted in English as well as Ibo. On 'Parents Days' the girls performed Ibo dances as well as English Country dances and the Scottish Reel, and they were encouraged to dress in their native attire whenever possible.

There was no wonder therefore that Miss Hill welcomed

Mazi Mbonu Ojike, the 'Boycott King' to address the girls on the Ibo language. He arrived at the school, wearing a jumper and a piece of 'jorge' tied round his waist. To the girls who had some foreign influence through Christianity in their elementary schools, Mazi Ojike's appearance was a bit odd. Some would have preferred him to have worn an English suit; others said he was projecting our culture and praised him for doing so.

Mazi Mbonu Ojike spoke eloquently in Ibo without adulterating it with spices of the English language. He maintained that the Ibo language was rich and complete, and it was a pity that many schools did not offer it as one of their subjects for the Cambridge School Certificate Examination. He was conversant with the writings of Peter Nwana, especially his classic work, 'Omenuko'. Ojike's language was so rich in idioms and proverbs that the girls applauded him. He told him that the spellings in the Ibo language were easy compared to English. The English, he said, pronounced one thing, and wrote another. The reason for this, he said was that the English borrowed words from other languages, and 'got confused' with the spellings.

Mazi Mbonu Ojike's visit was the talk of the school for many weeks. Many girls became more interested in the Ibo language, especially Rose and Dora. They spent their time collecting Ibo proverbs and idioms. Rose even went as far as writing a story in Ibo and won the recognition of their Ibo teacher Miss Okeke, who they learnt came from the same area as Mazi Mbonu Ojike. The rest of the Ibo lessons in Rose's class that term were devoted to the visit of the Mazi who was so well learned and yet used the Ibo language as though he had never stepped out of his village. The girls were beginning to understand why their able Principal was keen on them learning their language and being able to discuss in it.

The Principal and her staff did not realise at the time that the visit of the 'Boycott King' had caused a mild sensation in the school. For some reason, Rose got more interested in the affairs of the colonial regime in Nigeria. She had managed to smuggle in copies of *The West African Pilot* into the School, and had read them avidly. Nobody knew how she got them. While Mazi Mbonu Ojike talked about the Ibo language and its importance in their education, he had referred though briefly and subtly to the time when the mantle of government would fall on their great leader, Dr. Nnamdi Azikiwe. Rose had asked a direct question, 'When will Nigeria govern herself?' Mazi Mbonu Ojike had dodged the question, and when Rose put up her hand to ask another question, the Mazi ignored her. It was thought at the time that it was Mazi Mbonu Ojike who sent Rose *The West African Pilot* regularly. Others 'thought the papers came through Miss Okeke. Nobody was sure, for before the end of the year, Miss Okeke resigned her appointment and went to America. The girls later learnt that she benefited from Dr. Nnuku Eziso's scholarship. But some girls doubted this. The more likely thing and the story believed was that the learned Doctor had come back to Nigeria in search of a wife. He had gone to the Grammar School, to lecture with the hope that he would have the opportunity to also lecture in ACMGS. He was told about Miss Okeke, whose mother was in fact a relation of Maji Okike's. When the doctor was turned down by the Principal, for the flimsy reason that he spoke not only 'bombastic English' but American English as opposed to the King's English, the Doctor begged Mazi Ojike to go to ACMGS and see Miss Okeke.

Mazi Mbonu Ojike had seen his relation, Miss Okeke and liked her, and said so to Dr Eziso . Miss Okeke's parents were approached, and they readily agreed that the learned Doctor should marry their daughter. They could not say 'no' to such a brilliant and scholarly Ibo gentleman who, it was rumoured at that time, dined and wined with the President of the United States of America; a man who had read all the books in Howard University, Washington D.C.; a man who was better read than the Americans themselves; a man who had reached the pinnacle of knowledge; and a man with a

25

mission, who so loved his fellow Ibos that he had won so many scholarships for them. No parent could resist such a would-be son-in-law.

Dr. Nwafor Orizu was renowned throughout the length and breadth of Ibo land and so were his compatriots who had found it expedient to return home to be of help to their brothers and sisters who had not seen the light, and were suffering from the yoke of colonialism. He and his patriots were patriotic enough to return. There were others like them who rather than go to the United States of America, God's own country, decided to go to the institutions in the home of their oppressors, the so-called mother country. What did these men think they were doing by going to look for the golden fleece from the people who held them in chains? Did they not know that they would continue to be the slaves of their masters; that they would never be liberated? They were right, for some of the people who went to Britain after their studies, had married white women and settled in England for good.

When Miss Okeke resigned, the girls thought that the person who would benefit again from Dr. Orizu's scholarship was not going to be Miss Onu, but Rose. This was because of the way she read the West African Pilot, and her arguments on colonial rule in Nigeria. Be that as it may, Rose was a serious minded girl and so were her friends, Dora and Agnes. She knew why she was in the School. After all, her father worked for the colonial government, and she saw how good the relationship between her father and the so called oppressors was. True, her father was rather aloof and a bit of a playboy. The white civil servants referred to him as a gentleman. When her father invited them to his home, Rose tried to listen to the conversations, but she could not follow, for they spoke through their noses. They drank a lot in those days and enjoyed themselves considerably. What struck Rose at the time was that none of the white people who visited her father's home came with their wives. Perhaps, Rose thought, that was why

26

her father had not married again.

However, Rose knew that her father was not interested in the mood of that time. He made fun of the people who returned from America and were making a lot of noise. Rose remembered that at one time, before she went to ACMGS a group had visited her village asking for money to fight the colonial regime. Her father was not impressed, and did not contribute money. But then after Rose's first two years in ACMGS, her father, through her prompting, admitted that the new breed of men were doing a good job, but that their task was an uphill one.

School went on as usual. After Miss Hill had spoken to the girls about the time wasted in writing boys, and particularly after listening to Agnes' problem, she became kinder and more helpful. She organised more outings with the Grammar School, for she and the teachers believed that the more the boys and the girls met and exchanged ideas, the less the girls thought of them, and concentrated on their lessons. So practically every term, both schools visited each other twice or three times a term. Discussion groups were organised by the teachers in which the relationships between boys and girls were discussed at length.

As far as Rose and Dora were concerned, they had found their future life partners in Ernest and Chris. Agnes knew that she was never going to marry Sam, so her letters were quite restrained. As for Comfort, her case was already a hopeless one. School boys did not take her seriously any more. She ignored them, and made friends with boys who had already finished their schooling and were working, or in institutions of higher learning.

The discussion groups centred around the kind of relationship that would exist between the boys and the girls. Miss Onu, who was not married, was of the opinion that it should be platonic clean and unencumbered by empty promises of the future. Susy agreed with her but added that writing to many boys at the same time was not a sin because they were still young, and who knew what the future would bring?

27

Comfort applauded. 'But you are quite notorious, Comfort,' Miss Onu said. 'You have overdone it. But remember, while I agree with what Susy said, what is important is not how many boys you write to, but what you say and do with them.' The girls roared with laughter. The girls dreamt so much and had many illusions of what life would be like in the future for them. Dora was going to be a good wife to Chris. Nothing would cause a quarrel between her and Chris. She would work and earn money, so food money would not be a problem. She would augment the food money with her own if it was not enough. She was not going to work during the first four or five years of her marriage until she had had about four children. Not working did not just mean being a mere house-wife. She would do other jobs, like sewing and baking.

Women would not be a problem either. Chris would love her, so much so that he would not look at any other woman's face as long as she was his wife. Men were tempted by women other than their wives, because the wives had neglected themselves. She was not going to be in that category. She would not only be a good cook, but a good wife who will keep the house clean, and not neglect her looks. She was not going to be like other women, who, when they had their first babies, stopped taking care of themselves, added weight, and forgot to watch their figures. She was not going to be like that. As soon as she had her baby, she would do exercises to keep her tummy down. She would mind what she ate so that she did not bulge in the wrong places. Nothing would make Chris lose interest in her. Nothing at all.

Rose had the same notion about married life. Ernest was a sweet and loving boy, very handsome and very particular about where he lived, what he wore, and what he ate. She would see to it that he lacked nothing. The fact that they came from the same area was an added advantage. There was not going to be a culture clash. Ernest knew her relations and she knew his own relations as well. Her own mother was dead, so, that worked even better, for they would have just one mother to take care of. Ernest was to do his Cambridge School Certificate that year. He would go to Yaba Higher College, and later read medicine. By the time he finished his course at Yaba, she, Rose would be finishing at ACMGS, and they would be married. Then if he wished to go abroad and read for his specialist degree, he would take her. She was not sure of what she would read when she went abroad, but whatever Ernest suggested would be all right. The United States of America was the one place she wished to go to. But then all depended on Ernest. He knew what was good for her.

The holiday they spent together had been wonderful. He had told her how much he loved her. He had even told his mother that Rose was the girl he was going to marry. They had even made a plan which they called a twelve year plan. In twelve years, they would marry and have ten children. Ten was Rose's idea. Ernest said ten was too many. But Rose said she could manage with ten children. She loved children. Ernest had merely smiled and thought of other things.

When Comfort heard all these things, she was sure the girls were insane. 'Who told you, you are going to do all these things you are planning? Look, Rose, when Ernest goes to Yaba Higher College, he will meet students of his own age there, go out with them, and propose marriage. He will not remember you. The distance is too much and you are too young. He will want someone nearby with whom he will discuss the latest lecture or the latest physics problem. Take my advice, you do not know at this stage whom you are going to marry. I do not know, nobody knows, except of course Agnes,' Comfort concluded.

'But how do you know?' asked Rose.

'Very easy. Have you seen her album? There is a photograph of a man in it she says is her uncle. That man is not her uncle. He is her fiancee. I can bet my life on it.'

'How did you know?' Rose asked in surprise.

'I know by intuition. I watch Agnes a lot especially when we talk about our boy-friends. She says nothing. She is

29

lukewarm about Samuel. And you remember, one Sunday, she had a visitor from Lagos who brought her a huge parcel. She hid that parcel in her box, and when we asked her, she said her visitor was her uncle. You were all taken in by it, not me. I know exactly what is happening.'

'You know the story of everyone in this school, Comfort,' Rose said.

'Not quite, I have my eyes wide open that's all, and I do not pretend like other girls. You remember that I was the one who suspected that Miss Okeke was going to leave us soon, and she did. Nobody told me, but I knew.'

'What then is your plan on leaving school?' asked Rose.

'Get a job, work two or three years, hook a man, get him to the altar. Have three or four children for him, and if he does not make it, leave him,' said Comfort.

'If he does not make what?' asked Rose.

'I am not going to continue to count pennies all my life. And marriage for me will not be for better or for worse. Only fools think of that. I am going to live life fully. If I am lucky and first land on the man who has already made it, all well and good. I could stay. But if not, I will be on the move.'

'You are going to marry for money then?' asked Rose.

'Who doesn't? My mother did.'

'You are not going to marry for love then?'

'Love? I want to marry someone who will take care of me. I want to marry a rich man. Love my foot.'

'What are you doing with all the boys you write to? Aren't you or aren't they attracted to you in that way?'

'In what way?' Comfort interrupted.

'I mean to marry Ernest. I mean it. I love him very much.' Rose said.

'And he loves you very much,' Comfort repeated.

'Of course he loves me. I have all his letters and he is . . .'

'Rose, don't be taken in by what you read in "True Romances." What I know, that is most likely to happen to us, I mean you and I, Agnes and Dora, is that Agnes will marry her "uncle" as soon as she is allowed to finish her schooling. As for us, anything can happen as far as marriage is concerned.'

'Who has been telling you all these things?' asked Rose, and before Comfort had time to reply, the bell for lights out went, and they raced to their dormitories.

Rose jumped into her bed after wearing her nightdress and covered herself up waiting for Miss Hill to come round and say goodnight to them. The dormitory was quiet. One could hear a pin drop on the cement floor. She came in like Florence Nightingale with her lantern.

'Good night girls'.

'Good night, Miss Hill. Sleep well, Miss Hill. "Laru ofuma", Miss Hill,' said the girls.

'Laru nu ka ngwere,' Miss Hill said in Ibo.

The girls roared with laughter. 'Thank you, Miss Hill. We shall sleep like lizards and not like rats,' said the girls.

But the 'Three Musketeers' did not sleep immediately. They were hungry. There was nothing to eat, but dry gari and coconuts. The senior girls had been murmuring about the poor food the contractor was buying, and had complained to the staff. The food improved a little, then became worse again. So without warning the younger girls, the prefects decided to go on hunger strike.

Miss Hill had dressed for dinner and was waiting for Miss Backhouse when she heard the prefects. The prefects were normally not appointed but nominated by the girls and then voted for. They were nearly always loyal to Miss Hill and the staff. She had weekly meetings with them where the affairs of the school were discussed. The prefects were asked to come in and as she opened the door for them, she was shocked to see the basins of food rejected by the girls at her door step. She was angry, but she held her temper and tried to pacify the prefects. The senior prefect spoke and when Miss Hill tried to speak again, she was so interrupted that she abandoned them in her sitting room and went to her bedroom. The prefects, after making so much noise, left the basins of food in her sitting room and went back to the

31

dormitories to report to the girls. The junior girls wept. They were hungry, they should have eaten the food before the prefects took it to the Principal. One of the girls, Janet by name, who was so quarrelsome, and who came from an area where matchets were used freely said that the only lesson that Misses Hill and Backhouse would be taught was beating. If the girls agreed with her, she would beat the two women up.

Rose, Agnes and Dora were so astonished that they began to cry. 'Please don't beat them up. Please whatever you do, don't beat them up. They have been good to us. They are so delicate, they could die. They have left their relatives and friends, their beautiful homes to come to this bush to educate us. Please, *please*.'

'Nonsense.' It was Comfort. 'Stuff and nonsense,' she repeated. 'Mind you,' she went on. 'I am not for beating them up. God forbid. But what I want to say is that they have not left their beautiful homes to come to Africa to educate us. What beautiful homes? Have you ever been to their homes? How beautiful are they? You have not been. They have a mission, they are missionaries. They took up the job voluntarily. Now you will soon tell us that they are celibate because of us. That is nonsense.'

'Comfort, please do be quiet,' Rose said. 'My father told me that Misses Hill and Backhouse and all the other white women the Anglican mission have in Nigeria are highly educated in the best universities in Great Britain. My father told me that no white woman will ever leave her home in Britain to live in this bush educating silly girls like us, with no good company, no electric light, no running water, and the bush infested with mosquitoes and tse-tse flies. Didn't you see Miss Backhouses's hands and fret the day we went on that expedition to collect wild fruits for our Botany lesson? Didn't you see how fresh she looked when she returned from her overseas leave?'

'I know you want to say that she was proposed to during her overseas leave and she turned the man down, and . . . .

32

don't laugh girls, I am serious. Rose thinks she is the only one who knows about the white people in Nigeria. Neither she nor any of us have ever been to Lagos, let alone take the boat across the Atlantic Ocean for Britain. And Comfort, I can boast that I am the only one here who has seen white people at close quarters apart from those here and from what my father says about them, they . . .'

'Leave your father out of this. We don't want to know what your father said and did not say. I am not for beating up Misses Hill and Backhouse' – and as she said this, she turned to Janet who had suggested the beating. 'Janet, we are not as uncivilised as your people. We do not carry matchets where we come from, so, we are not going to . . .'

'Who, who do you call uncivilised? Me? You call me uncivilised? You, Comfort, you wait here. You will witness my "uncivilisation" right here.' As she said this, she raced to the store, and got hold of a matchet.

'What do you think you are doing with that matchet?' a senior girl asked Janet.

'To cut off Comfort's head,' she replied sharpening the matchet on the cement floor of the dormitory.

The senior girl held her, 'Please, Janet, please. This is a Christian school. We are taught to be gentle, humble and human. We are taught, to "do violence to no man". Please, *please.*'

'What right has Comfort, that silly and uncouth girl to call my people uncivilised? From what home does she come from? Is her home better than my own? Look at her, her people went about stark naked not long ago. It was only when the missionaries came that they taught them how to cover their nakedness. I want to get hold of that Comfort and cut off her foul tongue, so she won't insult anybody again in this school. Stupid girl who has been written off by all the boys schools in the whole of Nigeria. What man in his good senses will ever marry her?'

'I suggested that we should beat up these women, so they learn to respect us. So they feed us properly. At home my

33

father can eat a whole leg of a goat at one sitting, and I come here and beg for a tiny and miserable piece of meat. And now the prefects have called for hunger strike without thinking of what we will eat. Now I'll go to bed hungry. Witches will bring me food while I am asleep. Leave me to cut off Comfort's head.' She went on sharpening the matchet.

Rose, Dora, and Agnes took Comfort to Miss Onu's house for protection. She spent the night there, and was seriously shaken. Miss Onu assured her that Janet was merely joking, that she did not mean her threat.

'I know her, Miss Onu. I know her background. She meant everything she said. If you allow her, she will carry out her threat. She will cut off my head, Miss Onu. She is like that. I have seen her cut a huge snake into two with her matchet. She uses her matchet as you and I use our pens and pencils. Oh, I am so scared.'

Miss Onu assured her that she was safe. She was really sorry for Comfort. Everybody knew Comfort and her foul tongue, but she exuded sympathy and love towards others in any difficulty. At this time, she became as mild as a lamb ready for slaughter. She spoke quietly and clearly, and was humility herself. After the difficulty had been overcome, she was her boisterous self again.

However the strike and the behaviour of the girls were taken seriously by the school. Miss Hill did not come round as usual to say goodnight to the girls. The five thirty bell did not go in the morning. The girls were in serious trouble. The authorities were now on strike, and what were they going to do?

They managed to do the usual morning chores, had breakfast and went to their classes for registration. There were no teachers in the class-rooms. Everywhere was as quiet as a graveyard. 'We are in hot waters,' the girls whispered. 'They are going to send all of us home,' some said. Others hushed them up. No teacher was in sight. Comfort whispered to Dora that she had a good night's sleep at Miss Onu's. 'I don't know what my father would say to me if Miss Hill sends us home,' Agnes thought. 'I might be a bride before I know it,' she went on thinking. 'And for what reason? For bad food? What was wrong with that food served us the night before? It was not as bad as the food we have been eating all along.'

Miss Hill reported the incident to the teachers, tearfully. The teachers saw that she was very upset. The behaviour of the prefects was to say the least, appalling. She did not expect the prefects to behave in such a crude and uncouth manner. Could it be possible that the girls, well selected from good Christian homes, could come here *bush*, and leave here *bush*? When the school was founded, the foundation was laid on good Christian norms. The emphasis was on good behaviour, cleanliness, godliness and humility. 'I thought I was bringing up well brought up and educated girls entrusted in my care,' she said. 'I was very proud of them until last night. If the prefects behaved in this way, how will the rest of the girls behave? If they can exhibit such crudity in the school, what will be their behaviour outside the school?'

The Nigerian teachers pleaded, made unconvincing excuses, though they condemned the girls' behaviour. Miss Hill should impose punishment on the whole school as she thought fit.

On that occasion finally, the bell rang, and the girls heaved a sigh of relief. At least something was happening, good or bad. The suspense was terrible. The girls were summoned to the chapel, not the assembly hall. The matter was too delicate, too important to be discussed in the assembly hall. When a girl grossly misbehaved, Miss Hill or Miss Backhouse usually sent her to the chapel to pray, for the girl misbehaved because she was far from God. In the chapel, she would pray to God, and in doing so, be near God, repent, and be forgiven.

The chapel was built with mud, which was got locally. The mud-wall was dwarfed so that air would flow in undisturbed. The roof was high, and made with local thatch. There were no chairs but benches made with mud, in rows on both sides of the building, leaving a space in the middle for one to pass through to the altar. The altar was elevated like a platform. There was a table, and a wooden cross on the table. On Sundays, a white table-cloth covered the table in the altar. Miss Backhouse arranged the flowers on the altar.

To this chapel, the girls went to face their Principal. The fact that the whole school was involved did not lighten the problem. They had never been summoned in that way before. Miss Hill first of all asked the girls to pray quietly and ask God's forgiveness. Then the text of the day was read from the New Testament. Then she preached a short sermon on Christianity and what was expected of Christian children. She also gave them a short history of the ideology, if one could call it so, behind the foundation of the school. Then she enumerated all the misdemeanours of the girls since she was the principal of the school. And then the hunger strike. If there had been a report a week or two before the shameful behaviour of the girls, she and her staff would have talked to the food contractor as usual, and something done. Why did the girls go on hunger strike without warning her? And why should the prefects insult her by placing basins of food at her door step, and even in her sitting room?

She choked, waited for some time and when she regained her composure she went on again. She had had a long meeting with the staff who were equally shocked by the behaviour of the girls, and who had been asked to punish them. What punishment was she going to adopt? She had thought about it all night but had not arrived at any worthwhile punishment.

Could it be all right for her to send down the girls for a period so they would realise the gravity of their behaviour. Agnes burst into tears and all eyes were turned on her. 'Poor child,' thought Miss Hill and waited for her to stop crying.

If it were in the assembly hall, some girls like Comfort or even Rose would have put up their hands to speak, but this was not allowed in the chapel, the Holy of Holies. Whoever argued with a pastor while he preached? The pulpit was his

36

domain, his privilege. He could stay there hours talking sense or nonsense and the congregation was obliged to sit and listen. If your thoughts were on one particular problem, you were lucky, but if your thoughts wandered like Rose's own you almost died of boredom. But somehow Agnes' outburst brought a kind of relief, even if it were a comic one. The girls shifted on the mud benches. How uncomfortable the mud benches were, and they were taught to sit straight and not to slump as they sat. Because of this interruption the girls had time to look around them and to stretch and yawn.

Comfort wanted to talk very badly. She thought it was unfair. The prefects did not tell them they were going on hunger strike. If they did, she would have said no, and even reported to the Principal. Now they were being punished by the Principal. The prefects should own up, they should take the blame.

Miss Hill went on, when Agnes stopped crying. She must have remembered Agnes' problem. Sending the girls home was not going to solve the problem. Some girls' parents lived very far away, and before they were sent home, their parents must know, and they were bound to ask why. Some girls like Agnes would not even go home to their parents, and the school would be in trouble.

The punishment was that there would be no classes for the day and the girls would write an apology to Miss Hill and the staff for their misdemeanour. The prefects were no longer to be prefects. For the rest of the year, the principal and staff of the school nominated the girls they thought fit to be the prefects.

The incident of the hunger strike was not quite forgotten when there was a commotion in the dormitory next to Rose's. What was the matter? Rose was curious, so she got out of bed, went through the box room, opened the door slightly and heard two senior girls quarrelling. 'You wait until we go to the classroom tomorrow, and I'll show you that you copied my answers during the test!' That was Susy.

'Please be quiet. Miss Hill has not quite forgiven us yet.

37

We mut be of good behaviour at least until the end of the term, please,' said another senior girl. 'And . . . and you wait until Miss Hill comes, and I'll tell her that you have been eating all the food meant for the girls with your friends. I was there when the food contractor brought some fresh fish today for the evening meal. You cooked it and invited your friends after the evening meal and ate all the fish with them. You used the meat which was already bad to cook for the girls,' said OBY.

'You know you are lying. Rose, Dora and Agnes can bear me out. We were not given the fresh fish. It was meat for the other house, not our house. So stop your nonsense. You have been copying my work all along, and when I confronted you, you talk of what you do not know . . .'

The girls in the dormitory roared with laughter. Rose wondered why they were laughing. The accusation was quite serious. OBY was right. She saw the fish, and thought it was going to be used for the evening meal. Then when it was time to cook, Susy asked them to use the old meat. Dora was a bit surprised but she said nothing. Who must have told this girl? She knew she did not talk. It could not have been Agnes because she was not there when the food contractor brought the fish.

'You are lying, you are lying,' filled the air, and outside was Miss Hill waiting for the noise to die down. Rose slipped back to her bed and covered herself up. When the noise did not die down immediately, Miss Hill knocked at the door, and said, 'Girls, please be quiet. I have waited here for over ten minutes. Please be quiet.'

'You greedy girl. Perhaps you don't have fresh fish in your home, that is why you eat the one meant for all the girls,' shouted OBY, and the rest of the girls roared with laughter, and by so doing encouraged the girl to say more. That was a juicy gossip. But it was quite serious after the strike incident. Why were the girls laughing? The strike incident taught them a hard lesson. During assembly after the strike, Miss Hill had devoted at least six minutes to two great sins, greed and waste.

38

The girls detested greed. Anybody who displayed this tendency was written off. She was not fit in the first place to be admitted to ACMGS. The school was a christian school where the teachings of Christ were taught diligently, and practised. Why, why did Susy of all people steal their food? Why did she and her friends deprive them of their fresh fish? Fresh fish was a rare commodity in the diet of the girls. If they were given fresh fish once a term, they were lucky.

'And . . .' OBY went on. 'Don't tell us that you ate the fish with Rose and Co. You did not. Rose and Co had already gone to play games when you cooked the fish and hid it from them. And you are supposed to take care of the girls. You are supposed to be their "mother". They have confidence in you, and here you are cheating them. Why did you not let them partake of the fresh fish? They do all the work for you. You sleep while they are up. Even when there is no water, the girls go down to the stream to fetch water so as to cook, and you stay with your friends, playing "big madam". Eating the fish meant for the whole house. You should be ashamed of yourself. Shame on you. Shame on you. Sweet mouth.'

'Please be quiet girls, I am still waiting,' said the gentle voice of Miss Hill.

'But Miss Hill, Susy must . . .,' she did not finish.

'Will you be quiet,' said Miss Hill. 'The rule of the school must be obeyed which is that when the lights out bell goes the first time, all girls are expected to go to their dormitories and prepare for bed. When the second bell goes, all lights are out, and everybody lies down waiting for the mistress on duty to come and say good-night. All this time, there should not be any talking from anybody. You should set a good example, Mercy. You should know better.'

'Susy started it and . . .'

'Will you be quiet, Mercy.'

The next day, the staff met. Mercy and Susy were invited. The accusation was quite true. Susy was sent down for a week.

Chapter 3

As the next three years passed, Miss Hill saw the girls God entrusted in her care preparing to face the adult world. Their secondary education was coming to an end. What kind of children were they going to be? What kind of world were they going to work in? A hostile world? Were they going to remember all the Christian teachings? Were they going to be greedy and undignified in manner? What kind of women would they be?

They had grown up, loving one another. Were they going out into the world to contribute to the upliftment of mankind? Or were they going to be selfish and self-seeking? Was it not time for her to go back to her home and continue the good work there and leave the scene for the new breed of educated Nigerian women? There had been more and more talk about self-rule and even independence. How long were they going to hold on to power in Nigeria? Perhaps she would see this set through to their Cambridge School Certificate examination and then go home. In her heart of hearts she loved this set of children. She could not believe that it was she who went to Port Harcourt to invigilate the entrance examination that brought them to the school. She had gone home three times since then, but still time had passed quickly.

As she sat in her office filling in the registration forms for the examination, she wondered how the girls would perform. She was sure that they would make it. She had received a letter that day which said that Janet was going to be married. She was going to announce it to the girls during assembly.

She was glad that she had finally convinced Agnes' father to allow Agnes sit for her Cambridge School Certificate and then marry after the examination. She would be better equipped to face the world if she had that essential certificate. She assured Agnes' father that she would pass very well. That had made Agnes so cheerful in her final year. She read more than all her friends. It seemed to be her last chance of formal education, and she was determined to make a good grade. The girls were also full of speculation about the forthcoming examinations. 'Don't you hear what the staff are saying?'

'What are they saying, Comfort?' asked one.

'Oh, you have not heard? They are saying that we are not as bright as the set before us. That if we have a fifty five per cent pass, it will be a good result.'

'No, they have not said that,' said Dora and Agnes.

'Take my word for it, they said it. I overheard them at the staff meeting.'

'One day you will be caught eavesdropping,' the girls warned Comfort.

'They won't catch me. But tell me before we start swotting. I envy Janet you know.'

'Look, don't distract us. If you don't want to read, go and sleep. Didn't you say sometime ago that your ambition was to get your certificate, work for two or three years and hook a man . . .'

'Yes, I know, but . . . Look, thinking of it now, do you think Misses Hill and Backhouse will ever marry?'

'Why not?' asked Rose. 'If men propose to them.'

'What men will propose to them?' Comfort asked.

'Missionaries like them, who are not like Roman Catholic priests. Bishops get married in the Anglican Church,' said Rose.

'And is it true that the female missionaries choose not to marry?' Comfort went on.

'How do we know, Comfort? I think that some women choose not to marry so as to do the work of God,' said Rose.

41

'No, I am told that no woman chooses not to marry unless she was badly disappointed by a man or something like that,' said Agnes, who was more relaxed now about discussions on marriage.

'We are wasting precious time talking about marriage when we have work to do. What I know is that I am going to marry after being trained. I may even go to the University, I don't know. It all depends on Ernest,' Rose said.

'She is mentioning Ernest again. Won't you forget Ernest?' said Comfort.

Agnes put in, 'Rose is right you know. However I am seizing this opportunity to invite you all to my own wedding at Easter.'

'A year from now?' asked everybody.

'Yes. You know of course. I was hiding it all the time. But now that I have been allowed to reach Form Six, I might as well tell my friends.'

'Well, Rose and Dora let's make haste otherwise we shall be a bunch of spinsters like Misses Hill and Miss Backhouse,' said Comfort.

'God forbid,' the girls said.

They read on for the Cambridge School Certificate. They would all pass. They were told that the examination was not all that difficult. What was difficult was its preparation. If the previous set made seventy five per cent, they would improve on their performance and make eighty five or ninety per cent.

It was Sunday, the girls had returned from church, and as Rose was changing into her house dress, Agnes and Dora came in looking rather tired. 'You know one thing I am not going to miss in this bush school is the village church. It is high time the congregation told these cathechists that they have to shorten their uninteresting sermons. Imagine listening to Miss Hill's sermon, and then that village cathechist's. He spoke for nearly one hour today. I had my watch on,.' Dora said. 'And the singing. You have forgotten the singing,' said Agnes.

'What I hate so much about that church is that horrible anthem they sing. Hasn't anybody told them that they sing out of tune? And why on earth must that cathechist suddenly switch into poor English language when the congregation except us, do not understand English?'

'This year will end it all. Are you two going to the classroom? I am going there to write to Ernest,' said Rose.

'Me too, I am going to write to Chris,' said Dora.

'And I will write "uncle" in inverted commas then my father,' said Agnes. 'Rose and Dora, you should pray for me about this marriage. I don't know if it will work. And I do want to go to the University to read, graduate and work. This marriage is going to upset everything.'

'Must you really marry this man?' asked her friends.

'Of course. I have no choice in the matter. All is set – Easter of next year.'

'In that case, we shall attend your wedding,' said the girls.

'Thank you, if there will be a wedding that is,' said Agnes and left them.

Dora and Rose went to the classroom and there Rose wrote to Ernest while Dora wrote to her Chris. Chris was already working and sent Dora expensive presents. But he did not visit her in the school. Ernest did not work, he gained admission to Yaba Higher College to read medicine. It was the institution that the brains of the country went to in those days. You had to be exceptionally brilliant to go there. And the first thing that Ernest told Rose on reaching the college was that there were three girls in the college, and that if she worked very hard, she would come to the college as well.

Thereafter he wrote infrequently to Rose and when the long awaited reply arrived, it was very scanty. But he always gave excuses. He was very busy reading. The college was highly competitive, and if he failed his examinations, he would be sent out and where would he go next, and what would happen to their twelve year plan?

On receiving this kind of letter, Rose would day dream for days. She would read and read the letter until she could repeat the words by heart. She would then reply and tell him that she understood. That she would continue to write him every week whether he replied or not because she loved him so much. She would tell him that she was working very hard and by the grace of God, she would make a good grade in the School Certificate. She congratulated the three girls who could compete with the boys. She knew she was not as brilliant as they were, but she would read hard. If they did it, she too would do it.

Dora wrote the same kind of letter to Chris, professing her love for him. She was not all that ambitious. She was content with the Cambridge School Certificate. As he was already working, they would get married as soon as he, Chris, was ready. She did not envisage any problem with her father and she was sure that Chris did not have such problems either.

When the bell for lunch went, Dora and Rose went hand in hand to the dining room where they saw Comfort sulking. 'Where have you been?' she asked, and before they had time to reply, she went on, 'I have been everywhere looking for you. I received a letter on Friday from one of my boy-friends. I put it under my pillow and forgot all about it. I discovered it after church and I read it. It was quite an extraordinary letter and . . .' She stopped. The dining room was now filling up with girls.

'After the meal,' said Dora and Rose.

'What kind of girl is Comfort?' Rose asked herself several times as she was eating. The fact that she received a letter on Friday and forgot about it, and saw it by chance on Sunday was extraordinary. She is not serious with anybody, and will have herself to blame, she thought.

So when the meal was over, Agnes joined them and they went to the dormitory. 'If I receive Chris' letter and I don't read it immediately, the world stands still,' said Dora. Rose, Agnes and Comfort laughed at this apparent exaggeration.

'Well, this boy is not special. He is one of the boys I met during one of our holidays. He is in Form Six and like us,

44

preparing for the examination. I was not particularly keen on him. He talked book all the time. You know what the Government College, Umuahia boys are like. They are bookworms, and are not as mature as the boys of the Grammar School. So for want of any other company I allowed him to visit me though I did not return his visits. He did not even ask to take me to the cinema. Well, to cut a long story short, he wrote, here is the letter. There are one or two hints on the English paper. He said that for essay writing, he thought one of the topics would be "Trees" and "A Long Journey". For geography we should study everything on River Basins, The Equatorial Forests and Longitude and Latitudes. For English Literature, we should memorise the great speeches in Shakespeare's Richard II . . . and . . . What am I doing, here is the letter, read it.'

The next day in class the girls asked questions based on what they read from Comfort's letter, and their teachers revised those topics with them. The girls agreed it did not mean that they were not going to read any other topics outside the ones on this strange letter. Agnes was the only one who was quite sceptical about Comfort's source of information. Comfort had a way of collecting information. In a short time, they forgot all about the topics and revised generally as their teachers taught them to do.

As the examinations were fast approaching, the girls began to read after lights out though they were warned not to do so. But the fear of failing was ever present.

So they had to read extra. They bought candles, and torch lights for swotting after lights out. Rose, Dora and Agnes 'ghosted' at the dead of night in a disused carpenter's shed. This was done very secretly because, if they were found out, they would be in serious trouble. But the final year students were never found out. The whole school conspired to keep 'ghosting' a secret from the authorities.

It must have been Comfort who was sent copies of Questions and Answers on History and Geography. She brought it to class and unfortunately for her, Miss Backhouse saw them. She was furious. That was exactly how not to pass an examination. Such books were harmful. She and Miss Hill had preached and preached to the girls that that was not the right way to read for an examination. Miss Backhouse had made it a point not to give the girls notes on her subjects. As a matter of fact, hardly any teacher in the school gave notes to the girls. Lessons were taught, and each girl made her own notes, as the teacher emphasised points and wrote them on the blackboard. She would have sent Comfort to the Chapel but for the intervention of Miss Hill.

Just before the school went on holidays and before the Cambridge School Certificate examination began, Miss Hill announced to the school that she was leaving them for good at the end of the year, and that Miss Backhouse was going to be their Principal. The girls received the news with mixed feelings. It came to them as a surprise. Hitherto the girls heard rumours of such things. So this gave way to wild speculations. Why was she going home so abruptly? Why was it kept a secret? Was she recalled by the authorities in England? Was she going to be married? Nobody had answers to those questions, and they dared not ask. But they were genuinely sorry that their Principal was leaving the school. The girls could get nothing at all from Miss Backhouse who said very little about Miss Hill's impending departure.

'We are forgetting the most important thing,' said Agnes. 'Exam or no exam, we must give Miss Hill a befitting send off.' Everybody agreed with her. The girls went to work, and in a matter of days, they had organised what they called an 'Evening of Events'. They set out to act out the entire ten years of their school. Miss Hill, Miss Backhouse and the entire staff marvelled at the manner the girls acted at the direction of the Form Six girls. They were impressed by the information they gathered and especially at the little girl in orm Two, who acted the part of Miss Hill. As the play went on, the history of the whole school began to unfold, the difficulties, and the insurmountable problems were all brought to light. What pleased the staff greatly was the sequel. The girls in the early years of the school were in the habit of reporting incidents without proof. And Miss Hill always told them that whatever they said must be substantiated. The girls acted an incident in which the head cook in the school's third year had reported to Miss Hill that the 'agidi' bought by the food contractor was bad. Thereupon Miss Hill followed her to the kitchen and asked her to unwrap the 'agidi'. The girl unwrapped one, and it was good, she unwrapped the second and it was good, the third, the fourth, they were all good. Miss Hill stood looking at her. 'What then?' she must have asked. The girl began to stammer in Ibo, 'fa si . . . fa si . . .' Miss Hill cut in, 'fa si, fa si you ought to see with your own eyes.'

The whole school roared with laughter and clapped and clapped for the two girls who had performed so well. Then the whole school sang a farewell song to Miss Hill. In the song, they told the life history of Miss Hill, and the refrain was

'Dear Miss Hill teach us your Maths,
Trala trala la la'

The 'night' was touching. Some girls said Miss Hill wept. At the end, Miss Hill spoke to the girls. As usual she was brief and to the point. She had had the most enjoyable time of her life in ACMGS. She regarded the girls as her own children. She had spent ten years in Nigeria, and she felt it was time for her to go back home, look after her aged mother and continue missionary work in England or anywhere.

She was proud to see the Form Six girls almost through to their examination. The certificate mattered, no doubt, but what mattered most was the Christian education the girls were given in ACMGS. She mentioned many old girls who were successful in the community they were in, and said the school was proud of them. She told them that they would appreciate their lives in ACMGS only when they had left it, because the old adage that school days were the best was true.

47

She told them they were going to encounter so many obstacles in the world at large, but they were not to be disillusioned because the world was not a bed of roses. She went on to tell them that their own world was quite different from the world in which she and Miss Backhouse came from. And therefore they should have an open mind about marriage and the raising of families.

She was happy that amongst the present form six girls she could see future graduates in English, History and nearly all the subjects, who would take over from where she and her teachers had left off. She could also see future stateswomen amongst them who would be in politics and thus shape the destiny of their country, Nigeria, She said, though perhaps unnecessarily, that she was not pleased at the way politics was going in the country and added that she feared for the political future of Nigeria. She warned them that it was too soon for Nigerians to advocate for independence. Independence, she said would come, but that the people must be prepared for it. To be prepared was not just building big government houses and mansions but to be prepared in spirit. Independence she told the girls did not mean that all the white civil servants should leave Nigeria and go home, so that the new breed of educated Nigerians should take their places. That was not the meaning. The meaning of independence was awareness of Nigerians to their responsibilities in government.

When she went home, she was going to pray for peace in Nigeria. She would pray for the new breed of Nigerians to have the wisdom and integrity to manage the affairs of Nigeria. The new breed of leaders should make the people aware of the burden of independence. They should not only emphasise the good things that would come after independence, but also the almost insurmountable problems with the advent of self-rule. She was not happy with the trend of events. There was too much confrontation in the newspapers especially *The West African Pilot*. The leaders must remember that they would make more impact and progress if they

48

adopted the policy of less haste and more speed in politics.

Miss Hill who spoke Ibo language fluently reminded the girls of the Ibo proverb which said that the person who ran, and the other who walked would eventually arrive at the same prearranged destination. Nigeria was a great country with many tribes and languages, and diverse customs and cultures; her future depended on the new breed of leaders, and from the utterances of the leaders, she did not think Nigeria would be as great as she would have been.

The Form Six girls were going to bear the burden of the change that would eventually take place. They would be called upon to man the civil service on account of their education. It was a privileged position which they were going to fill. Were they going to be the servants of the people, or masters? Were they going to manifest their Christian upbringing by shunning bribes and all the corruptions that would be inevitable as soon as the colonials left for their homes? If the husbands of the girls filled these positions, were they going to influence them not to take bribes.

The girls murmured. They had discussed bribery many times during their current affairs periods. Some girls pointed out that the problem of bribery was that there were more people ready to bribe than those ready to receive. Comfort had asked a question for those who said they would never offer or receive bribes, nor would they allow their husbands to do so: 'If your husband or your father or brother were faced with a jail sentence, and you were asked to offer a bribe to the magistrate or the registrar or the court-clerk, so he would falsify proceedings and evidences, and thus be freed, will you allow him to go to jail and live with that stigma all the days of your life?' Nobody could answer that question. Rose had said that if she knew that her husband received a bribe or a gratification, she would ask him to return the bribe; if he refused, she would divorce him. 'It is easier said than done,' the girls said in unison. One of the girls said, 'I like how Rose put it. Remember she said "if I knew". I am telling her that she will never know.' Rose had protested.

'My husband will tell me. Oh no, Ernest must tell me. Why should a husband or a wife hide anything from his or her spouse? When you are married, you become one in body and in spirit. I will never hide anything from Ernest, and I am confident that he will do the same. And besides, if a wife is observant she will know whether her husband is taking bribes or not.'

'How will she know?' asked the girl.

'She will know from the company her husband keeps, what her husband brings home, like clothes, drinks, gifts and so on. She will . . .'

'Will it shock you,' the same girl went on, 'if I told you that many wives do not know where their husbands work, to say nothing of what they earn.'

'And while we are on this, I want to tell you a funny thing that happened in our yard,' continued Comfort.

'I must have been in elementary four at the time. This man worked with the railways in Port Harcourt and lived in our yard. One day he asked my mother to make a wedding dress for his wife. "Are you about to be married?" my mother asked. "No," the man replied, "she is just a little girl". My mother was somewhat confused, but said she would like to see the girl so as to take her measurements. The bridal dress was made, then the wedding. The girl came to live with her husband in our yard. The husband treated her very well. What the young bride loved so much was Ovaltine and her husband always made sure that there was Ovaltine in the house. But then the man suddenly lost his job. Ovaltine and other delicacies were in short supply for sometime, and afterwards disappeared completely from the home of the husband and his new bride. What did the bride do? One morning, she disappeared. A week later, her father brought her back. Her reason for leaving was that her husband hated her for he no longer gave her Ovaltine to drink.' The girls roared with laughter. 'I ask you,' Comfort went on, 'why didn't her husband tell her that he had lost his job? Because if he did she would leave him all the same. Which is what I am saying that spouses whether educated or not cannot, all the time tell the whole truth and nothing but the whole truth to one another. So talking about bribe and no bribe, you and I will never know whether our husbands indulge in it or not. All we pray is that they may not be so disposed, and if they are, will not be caught. For if they are caught we will bribe to save them from jail and disgrace?

Miss Hill in her valedictory speech reminded the girls that as Christian children, they should show a good example for all to emulate. It was not what people said they were that they are, but what they are themselves. The friends they made in ACMGS were going to last them a life time if only they would keep in touch with their friends when they left the school. Again the girls should keep in touch with the school and be interested and involved with whatever their school was doing.

A senior girl gave a vote of thanks. Miss Hill was so overwhelmed by the night. She had little to say. All had been said through the acting put up by the first year girls. Miss Hill had spoken, it was left to them to remember her words of wisdom.

The next day the girls came out to wave goodbye to their Principal. A black car had arrived from Port Harcourt that morning. As Miss Hill went into it, the girls and the teachers waved goodbye. Some girls ran after the car, waving and waving until it was out of sight. Agnes, Dora, Comfort and Rose were among the girls who followed the car. Exhausted, they returned to their classroom. There was just one more hurdle, the Cambridge School Certificate examinations.

Chapter 4

Agnes

Agnes got married even before her Cambridge School Certificate result came out. (She passed in grade one.) The wedding took place in Lagos and Rose who was doing her post secondary course in Queen's College attended. Since Agnes had no mother, her step-mother organised the wedding.

Rose did not like Agnes' wedding dress neither did Agnes who looked so miserable on her wedding day. She could not even smile at Rose when she saw her among the crowd. Crowd? No, there was no crowd as such. There were just a few people, and Rose could count them. There were a few women whom Rose thought were the relations of Agnes' step-mother. They did not stop chatting behind her even during the church ceremony. She heard one of the women saying to the other: 'I endorse what Cecilia is doing. The sooner she gets her out of the way, the better for her. She sought my advice, and I gave it to her, "Marry her off as soon as possible, so she will be busy with her own family and won't bother you with yours." All that money spent on her to get education is now gone down the drain because of Agnes' stubbornness.'

'What do you mean?' asked the other woman.

'She insisted on getting a piece of paper before getting married, and her husband, that long suffering man had to wait all those years – a mere piece of paper, can you imagine?'

'And do you blame her?' asked the other one.

'I don't blame her,' she answered her own question. 'A lot

is changing. Our children will have to get that important piece of paper before they get married. I have told my daughter, she must have it. I don't have it and that is why Papa Emeka behaves in such an atrocious manner to me. He seems to tell me during some of our quarrels: "If you can't take it, go." Then I think – where will I go to with seven children? So I stay. But if I had that piece of paper which Agnes now has, I could have left him and gone to study.'

'Study? That means going back to school. Mama Nkem, you must be joking. Back to school, to do what? Get another piece of paper? What happens after that? Marriage, of course. So why bother with book if you are eventually going to be married? My daughters will marry as soon as worthy suitors come their way. I will encourage all of them to marry, just have those three letters – M – R – S, just answer MRS, and you can do any other thing you wish to do. That's what I tell my daughters – I say, go and answer MRS then if you cannot cope with marriage, you can do other things.'

Rose listened as the marriage ceremony was going on. The conversation of the women was most intriguing to her. So there were mothers who could say such things to their daughters? The women went on. 'And tell me Mama Emeka, what does this man do?' asked Mama Nkem.

'Oh, that's another story. That's where I blame Cecilia. If Agnes were her daughter she would not have allowed her to marry an impostor.'

'An impostor?'

'Yes, an impostor. Well before I go into that, there is one thing I must say for Agnes' husband. He has been patient. He had wanted to marry Agnes when she was a little girl of ten years old, when Agnes' mother was alive. He paid Agnes' school fees both in primary and secondary schools. It was Agnes' mother who insisted that Agnes went to school in the first place. She did not like the man of course. But you know what our husbands are like. Once they are given money, they sell their daughters.

'The man was and is an impostor, that is an established

53

fact, but a well behaved and generous impostor. It was rumoured at one time,' and she lowered her voice, though it was loud enough for Rose's keen ears, 'that he was Cecilia's lover. So they said, I am not sure, I have no proof, but so I heard

'So he posed as a medical doctor. He is not a medical doctor, he is a dealer in drugs in one of the numerous markets in Onitsha. I do not know whether Agnes or her father knows. But as I told you, he is generous, and in our society, once you are generous, you are a good man, then . . . she, sh . . .'

Everybody stood up, as the bride and the bridegroom went to the vestry to sign the book. Rose looked round but there was nobody she recognised, so she sat down again, and the two women continued their yapping. 'For better for worse my foot,' said Mama Emeka.

'What do you mean?' asked Mama Nkem.

'I prefer our own native law and custom marriage. "For better for worse." Nobody bothers to uphold a marriage if things begin to go wrong.'

'I don't agree with you.'

'I am not asking you to agree with me. It is a fact. Our children will not take what we are taking from our husbands. Mind you, I am happily married to Papa Emeka. He is a wonderful person. But you know what I am talking about . . .'

The wedding march began, and the bride and the bridegroom came out hand in hand from the vestry. Agnes still looked unhappy. She was not smiling. Rose could see her husband clearly now. He was not as old as she had thought. He was quite handsome. The suit he wore was not bad at all. There was something fatherly about him, and that was a quality that Rose admired in some elderly men. He was full of smiles, nodding to guests on his right and left. What a contrast. He was happy. He had done it at last. He had married Agnes at last. He had dreamed of marrying her since she was ten years old. That dream had become a reality at last. She had made it already. She had passed the all important Cambridge School Certificate. And now Agnes and the certificate were his for keeps.

'Why, why does she look like that?' Mama Emeka went on.

'She is pregnant, can't you see, poor child,' Mama Nkem said. 'Of course, she is. Three months. A bad time for her. She must be feeling bad. Oh why didn't they postpone the wedding. No wonder she is looking like that. Poor girl.'

As the bride and the bridegroom approached them, Mama Emeka said aloud, 'Jisike, We are all behind you.' Agnes looked up, and saw Rose and could not help smiling. Rose could only see the awful dress clearly. To Mama Emeka she gave a bad look, unbecoming of a bride.

In front of the Church, few photographs were taken. Agnes insisted that she would take one with Rose. But when her husband wanted to join them after they had been taken, Agnes frowned and beckoned to other guests to join them. Mama Emeka saw it all.

'Nonsense,' she said to Mama Nkem.

'Who is she deceiving? She is pregnant. Who made her pregnant? Not her husband? Why is she behaving as if she does not like or want him? If there is anything I hate, it is pretence. I must see the end of it. Come let's go to the reception.'

Agnes called Rose and asked her whether she was coming to the reception. She was coming, and she told Rose that she would see her there. There was something she wanted to say to her.

They chose to have the wedding reception in a small but clean hotel in Yaba. The place was well laid out and Rose was happy at what she saw. As in the church, the guests were few. There were no long speeches, and there was enough for everybody to eat. Both salad, jollof rice and meat were served as usual. Mama Emeka and Mama Nkem stuffed food in their handbags. Rose watched in disgust. Why were people so greedy? Then she heard Mama Emeka quarrelling.

'Yes, I left my children to attend this wedding. I am Cecilia's friend and she invited me to come. I must take something to my children. Come, that girl over there, bring me some chin chin.'

'Mama I have to serve those over there,' said the little girl who had the misfortune of being singled out by Mama Emeka.

Mama Emeka got up, two steps got her the plate of chin chin from the girl. She emptied it into her head tie. 'Do you want some?' she asked Mama Nkem who said she wanted some. Mama Emeka left her seat and went inside the pantry where the food was kept, got a tray of chin chin and gave half to her friend and kept half for herself.

'I must drink something,' Mama Emeka said. So she went to the high table where Agnes' step-mother was sitting. 'Cecilia,' she said, 'I thought you invited us to come and eat and rejoice with you because your clever step-daughter is getting married. Why must we sit here for the past one hour without being served a soft drink, not to talk of food. We are going. We have had enough insult. My children will be hungry at home. I must go and cook supper for them, thank you, and as you know . . .'

'Please sit down,' Cecilia said, and left the high table. She soon came back. 'Don't worry Mama Emeka. This place is a hotel, not my home. The ceremony will soon be over and we shall go home and make merry. The Chairman will soon make the closing remarks.' Mama Emeka left with much displeasure.

It was time for Rose to go back to the hostel. There was no time for her to see Agnes who was now too unhappy to say anything to anybody. What was she to do? She was too shy to come near the bridal table, but she had to make the effort. She had to give her the present she brought for her. So she got up, and went to the table. When Agnes saw her, she burst into tears. She was so embarrassed that she left the present on the table and disappeared.

Agnes had her plans. She was a bit cold-blooded about it. She went to her new home, and in a short time got it under control. There was no doubt right from the word go, that she was the mistress of it. Her husband who loved and worshipped her, gave her a free hand to run the home the way she wanted to run it. He went to work every morning, and returned at night to find everything in order, his supper on the table. He ate, and after the meal, a chair was taken out for him to sit on and he breathed the fresh air. For they lived in two rooms in Ebute-Metta, and shared the kitchen, the toilet and the bathroom with three other families.

Agnes' neighbours were surprised at the way she organised everything. They did not know when she had her bath, when she went to the toilet or when she cooked. She had a little girl who ran errands for her, having sent away the boy who lived with her husband. The two relations who also lived with her husband were sent home, where they went to school. When her husband's brothers protested, Agnes' husband told them to mind their own business. He did not want anybody, brother or sister to trouble his new bride. His brothers were greatly offended. Agnes had taken over their brother with juju. Their brother did not know them any more.

In six months, Agnes had her first child which was a boy. Her husband was happy and there was much rejoicing in the family. She was not interested in the job her husband did. All she cared about was to see that his meals were ready at the right time. She took care of her baby, and when her husband left home each morning, and the morning chores were over, she read. Unknown to her husband, she had registered with Wolsey Hall in England for the Advanced General Certificate of Education examination. She did use their home address, and studied each lesson thoroughly.

Sleeping with her husband was nothing special. She felt nothing. She submitted herself like a lamb ready for slaughter and prayed that it should be over quickly so she would snatch some sleep and read her lessons at night while her husband snored. Sometimes in her relaxed moments, which were rare indeed, she wondered whether her husband enjoyed sex with her or not. She did not and she did not care.

57

All she cared for was her GCE Advanced level which would enable her if she passed, to get her intermediate Bachelor of Arts degree.

In 1952 the examination was taken in Nigeria for the first time, and Agnes got hold of past question papers. Within three years of her marriage, she had given her husband three lovely children, and in June of 1954 she sat for the GCE Advanced level in English and history. Agnes was an avid reader in school. She was one of the best brains of her class. Being a mother did not disturb her in any way. English and history were subjects which she could manage very well at home.

Before the results were out, she had had her fourth child, and when the result was out, passed history and English. Then she proceeded to read mathematics and geography on her own, at advanced levels as well. It was at this time that she had to let her husband know that she was studying on her own, but she did not tell him the nature of her studies. Her husband told her it was all right with him since she had given him four children, and he had nothing to complain about her. But when she told him that she had to go to a night school, Mr. Egemba became apprehensive.

'A night school? In this Lagos? I don't think it is right,' he said.

'It is right,' Agnes said. When he refused to allow her she refused to cook for her husband.

Mr. Egemba sent for Agnes' father and when he complained to him about what Agnes had done, Agnes' father took the side of his daughter. 'She has had four children for you. She wants to read and improve herself and you say no. What kind of man are you? How much money do you give her as food money or pocket money? Has she ever complained to you? Has she ever quarrelled with you? Has she not been a good wife to you? If she wanted to have men, how would you know since you are away all day? Has she asked you to pay for the evening lessons? You should count yourself lucky and blessed to have a wife like my daughter.'

That closed the matter. Agnes had her way. She enrolled at the University for evening classes in Yaba, and there she met and fell in love with Ayo Dele. Then the marriage began to go sour. One night Agnes returned home to see her step-mother in a most compromising position with her husband. She had suspected this relationship, but she had no proof. The relationship had begun when she was in school and that was why her step-mother had stepped up the pressure on Agnes' father that she should be married. But Agnes' father was fond of Agnes and refused to be so pressurised.

Agnes said nothing when she saw this. For days she did not go for her evening classes. She did not show any jealousy either and this worried her husband. When it seemed as if the incident had been forgotten, Agnes resumed seeing Ayo Dele again. Then one day, Mr. Dele asked her whether she would live with him and without thinking, Agnes said yes. 'But what about the children?' Dele asked. 'I shall bring my children with me,' said Agnes.

So Agnes left her husband in a most callous manner. He went to work as usual, and by the time he returned, Agnes had left with their four children. Agnes' father was heart-broken, and shortly afterwards, he died.

Ayo Dele did what he was expected to do. Though he did not go with Agnes to bury her father, he made adequate provision for his burial. At home, Agnes' in-laws were not at the funeral as was expected of them. Her step-mother was too dazed to be useful, though according to tradition, she had very little to do with her husband's burial. All she was expected to do was sit on the bare floor and weep her eyes dry whether she felt like weeping or not. But she did feel like weeping and she wept. After all, she had had a good marriage. Agnes' father was good to her and even loved her.

Agnes gave her father what they call these days a befitting burial. But she did not escape the criticisms of the people. She heard someone saying behind her back that she, Agnes killed her father by deserting her husband and going to live

59

with a man who could be her own father. Agnes smiled within herself in spite of her grief. Her husband, she thought, was old enough to be her grandfather, so why were they complaining?

At the end of her stay, she saw her step-mother, sympathised with her and told her that she could stay if she wanted to stay, but if she wanted to marry again, and she knew whom she had in mind, she was welcome. It was not surprising therefore when Agnes heard, about three years later that her step-mother was living with her husband in Ebute-Metta.

The story gave her much relief. She felt less guilty for deserting her husband now that her own step-mother had stepped into her own home. What impudence!

Ayo Dele was good to Agnes and her children. He had a wife and grown up children living in London. Originally, he was a Sierra Leonean, but because of his long stay in Lagos, he described himself as a Lagos man, though his wife and children were never forgotten. Like Agnes' husband, Ayo Dele treated her like a daughter. Agnes was ambitious and he was determined to see her through her GCE Advanced Level examination. She was a good pupil and with his devoted coaching and the extra mural classes, she sat for the examinations and again passed the two subjects at advanced levels.

'How does she do it?' people asked. Ayo Dele made it possible, not only by coaching her and giving her a home, but by taking full charge of her children, whom he regarded as grand children.

'You have to go to the university now,' Ayo Dele told Agnes after the results were out. 'You have qualified to be admitted to the University College, Ibadan with your four advanced level subjects.' Agnes said she wanted to read for her degree on her own. She could get a job as a teacher and while teaching study as she had been doing. Ayo Dele told her it would be better for her to go to a university. There was a lot of difference between a person who studied to obtain his degree at home and another who went to a good university. There was a lot the university could offer to someone apart from just a degree. The inter-relationship between the students and the lecturers, the university atmosphere itself. The confidence one derived from merely going to the university was worth a lot in adult life.

At first Agnes did not want to go to Ibadan. She had her young children to take care of, she could get a good teaching job in one of the numerous schools in Lagos, and read for her degree. And besides, who was going to pay for her in Ibadan? It did not seem as if Ayo Dele had given a thought to that. But Ayo Dele had indeed given a thought to all that. Agnes applied to the University College, Ibadan, and she was admitted to the Faculty of Arts in October of 1957.

Ibadan was tough for Agnes, but she read and read. She did not make much contact with the lecturers as Ayo Dele hoped she would. This was because she was too busy not only with academic work, but with her young children as well. For nearly every other weekend, she went to Lagos to be with her children. A nanny had been brought in to take care of the children while Agnes was in the University. She struggled with her examinations. Maths gave her quite a problem, but she tackled it with vigour and single-mindedness. She realised what Ayo Dele told her was true, that there was much to gain in a university and less as an external student. What worried her a bit was having to read for the intermediate examination again, for her four advanced level subjects taken in two sittings had earned her an exemption from inter-B.A. as they fondly called it at the time.

Agnes passed her intermediate examination which she was told was a scrape through. She needed to have just two marks to make it, but because she was studious and had a tremendous responsibility, the board of examiners passed her. When the finals came and she made it, some people in the examination board thought she deserved a second class degree. But again because of her performance in intermediate, she had just a pass degree (1961).

She returned to Lagos, and before she got a job, a sad thing happened. Ayo Dele suddenly died. Before Agnes could get herself together, Ayo Dele's children pounced on her 'home' and seized everything she had worked for. The 'bastards', as Ayo Dele's children referred to Agnes' children, were saved by the Nanny, who took them away before any harm could come to them. That was December 1961.

Agnes wept and wept. Where would she go to? Finding a job at the time was easy. She hadn't even thought of getting one. Ayo Dele was to have done that for her. He was the first man Agnes related to, the first man she loved. He was both a lover and a teacher and a father to her children. Was she not being punished for deserting her husband? Was she not being punished for being over ambitious? How many women of her age at the time thought of University education? Many of her class mates were content with nursing and teaching. Her husband, though she was not in love with him, was kind to her. He respected her, he loved her, if that was love. Perhaps in his own way that was what he felt. But then why was she so cold, so dead when both of them were together? And why did she have to have a lover who was not young? If she could not relate to her husband because he was old and not young like Sam in the Grammar School, what about Ayo Dele? He was old but she related to him. When he made love to her, she responded. So, what was wrong with her? And now Ayo Dele was no more. She did not even have the honour of burying him. That honour was reserved for his wife who would mourn him in public. Agnes would mourn her lover in private.

With the help of Nanny, Agnes rented a two bedroom flat in Yaba, and applied for a job as a teacher in a private school there. She taught mathematics and English in the school. But a year after, she decided to join the civil service at Enugu, and there she was appointed a Woman Education Officer in the Ministry of Education.

It was 1962 when she came to Enugu to live. Many political changes were going on in the country. At Enugu,

62

she could see the changes clearly. There were new brave men at the helm of affairs who were ministers, and new money and new privileges were all over the place. There were young graduates from Ibadan like herself who had gone into the civil service and who were throwing their weight around. Young girls in school were no longer safe in Enugu. The young parliamentarians and the secretaries thought that taking over from the British meant having licence to corrupt young schoolgirls and their mothers. There were so many working girls who lived with this brand of people, while their wives lived in the villages. To them independence meant living in the GRA – Government Reservation Area, taking over the positions of the British, driving cars like their colonial masters, but ignoring the grave responsibilities attached to the new positions. The British were not emulated by these new men. The civil service was still regarded as the white man's service, and therefore one could cheat the government, and boast about it, because it was a foreign government. This mentality persisted years after independence and this worried Agnes and some well meaning people like her.

Agnes threw herself into her job as if the job was her father's. She worked under the Assistant Chief Inspector of Education who, sad to say, had not too much confidence in people like Agnes, her education notwithstanding. As a result, Agnes' reports were ignored and her efforts not appreciated. But she persisted in putting into practice what she learnt at ACMGS.

Her boss had worked under the colonial masters for a long time, rising from messenger to the position which he then held. The presence of people like Agnes in the service annoyed him. Good things had come to them too soon, and he was envious in spite of the fact that had it not been for independence he would have been a mere secretary in one of the ministries.

However, Agnes was lucky to secure a home in the famous GRA where those who had made it in the fifties and early sixties lived when and after the colonial masters had gone. Her home was a big one with two large bedrooms and large verandahs. Mango and guava trees were everywhere. Agnes made it a point to see that the gardens were well kept. Since the house was furnished, she did not have to bother to buy furniture. What she required was soft furnishing and she managed to buy a beautiful rug for the centre of the sitting room, which was large enough to hold a hundred guests at a time.

Agnes now had a car which of course went with the job. She had to get a driver for a short while before she learnt to drive. Another privilege was being invited to cocktail parties given by ministers. But she did not like these parties very much, for according to her the people she met were dumb, they had nothing to talk about other than ask you how the car was behaving.

She did not work for a year when she was asked to go to Lagos for a course on adult education. She understood later when she accepted to go that she was chosen because she had lived in Lagos and knew her way well, not because she was interested in adult education. She was pleased. She would take all her children and they would see their father. She would meet her friends in Lagos. She looked forward to going.

In Lagos, she paid a visit to her husband. The house they lived in was the same. The chairs were the same. So her step-mother did nothing to improve it before she left her lover? Shame on her. It seemed as if time stood still. It seemed as if there were no changes around. Seven whole years had gone by and not seven days of it were felt in this place that was once home. Her husband was sitting outside as usual after the evening meal. He had seen a car being parked at the front door and had gone in to put on a jumper to wear before whoever it was came out of the car. As Agnes emerged, he recognised her, and frowned. Agnes came near and greeted him. Agnes never called him anything, she never referred to him by name when she lived with him. Now she called him Papa Emena, Emena being the name of her first daughter. 'Papa Emena, I am Emena's mother, I have come to greet you.'

'Sit down, my wayward wife,' he said. A blunt knife seemed to have been driven into Agnes' heart. She said nothing, but tears filled her eyes. If she blinked, they would flow to her cheeks. She was not going to blink. This man was not going to see her tears. She was proud of her achievements, and nothing this man said now would upset her openly. 'Sit down, child. Is that your car? It is a beautiful car. And the children, I hope they are well. Whether you answer my name or not, you are my wife and the children are mine. One day, you will bring them back to me. You cannot say they are not mine. They are mine. You had them in my home, under holy wedlock. So whether you committed adultery or not, having them was my responsiblity, they are mine.'

Agnes turned back and left. It was not so much what he said, as much as the way he said it which frightened her into rushing into her car and driving away. She did not expect him to say what he said. She had taken a lot for granted when she lived with him. He knew about Ayo Dele of course. Thank God he did not know that he was dead. Or did he know? Perhaps if she visited him again, he would tell her that her lover was dead, and that it served her right. But did Agnes think that she was going to be welcomed by her husband as the prodigal son was welcomed? As she drove away, she thought, 'Why, why on earth did I go to see him?' But her subconscious mind kept answering back 'Why not?, why not?'

The course was boring. Who told the Eastern Region Ministry of Education that she was interested in adult Education? She must look for a job while in Lagos. She of course went to the course all the same. As luck would have it, she saw an advert in the *Daily Times*. A firm called John Levis Production and Research Bureau wanted a graduate to work as an executive. The pay was good. The fringe benefits were excellent, a flat at Ikoyi, a car and extensive travel in

Nigeria. She took her application with her to the office. She was interviewed by the Personnel Manager, a handsome Englishman in his forties, and given the job on the spot.

Agnes went back to Enugu, resigned and came to Lagos with her children in January of 1964.

Chapter 5

Dora

When Dora left school, she trained as a nurse, qualified, worked for a short time and married Chris, her boyfriend in the Grammar School. Chris was working even when Dora was in ACMGS. He made no attempt to go to any institution of higher learning. He made no attempt to continue to educate himself. All he read was the newspapers, and all he discussed with his colleagues in the High Court where he worked, was how to be rich without actually working for it.

He loved the good things of life. He dressed well, ate well and talked big. His salary was of course not good enough for the kind of life that he led and so he took bribes. He was not the only one who took bribes in the Registry. His colleagues and his boss, the Chief Clerk, took bribes as well. However, he did it discreetly and warned his boys to do the same.

But the sad thing was that Chris did not heed these warnings. He took bribes always, and everybody knew about it. The only person who did not know was Dora, his wife.

Dora worked as a nurse until she had her fifth baby in 1959; thereafter she told Chris that she wanted to set up a bakery. She was not making good use of her talents at all. She told her husband she would do very well baking cakes and other delicacies for sale. She was tired of nursing, and she felt she was not going to be promoted to a nursing sister even if she worked for six years. This was because the Chief Nursing Officer at the time was a disgruntled spinster who lorded it over married women. It was said that she made it known to all married nurses, that they could do either of two

67

things, be a wife and stay at home or be a nurse and work in the hospitals full time. Therefore she saw to it that no married nurse, or nursing sister stayed in the same town with her husband. If a husband worked as a civil servant in Enugu, his wife who was a nurse was sent to Calabar. In some extreme cases, the wife was sent to the Cameroons when that country and Nigeria were one.

So far Dora has been lucky to be at Ikot Ekpene with Chris. She was lucky because she was a mere nurse. at the bottom of the ladder. Again the nursing profession did not suit her. She had taken on the training for the simple fact that Aba, where she did the training was close to Ikot Ekpene where Chris worked.

Chris was not enthusiastic about Dora's proposal, but he was not going to be in her way either. He did not know what it entailed, and he did not ask. So Dora went on with her plans. She bought the things she needed for the business, quit nursing and started baking cakes and making doughnuts. She sent them to be sold in the hospital, and because they were good, they were sold in no time. In a short time, people started placing orders for the cakes and doughnuts and the business began to grow. Soon Dora had to move to a new premises, because she could no longer use her own house. Then she started baking bread, and when that too was successful, she bought a van to transport her products. When Chris saw that she was making profits, he became interested and agreed to keep the books for her. This was welcome, for as Dora discovered, she made the money all right but she could not give a proper account of the business.

Chris kept an almost perfect account. He was the accounts manager as well as the Bursar. Soon, they bought a piece of land, and started building a house in Chris' home town. Dora worked and worked, made the money, while Chris spent the money as he said, judiciously. But while he did this, he still kept his job in the Registry, he still took bribes, he still wore the best shirts, and still loved the good things of life. His colleagues envied him. What a wonderful wife he had.

What a mother! What a business woman! Some compared Dora with their wives, and went home to beat up their wives for not being as successful as Chris' wife.

Chris of course boasted, 'How dare you compare your illiterate wife with mine! Mine went to school, yours did not. Mine speaks English, yours don't. So where lies the comparison?' His colleagues laughed, but the boasting was getting too much. Chris was making enemies for himself and for his family. His Chief Clerk invited him to his office one day and talked to him. 'I have been hearing reports against you. You have been so overbearing. You have been rude and arrogant to your colleagues, and you have to do something about it before you become too unpopular.'

Chris thought of the advice seriously and even mentioned it to Dora who was horrified. Dora had been so busy making money and taking care of the children that she did not know this side of Chris. 'Why not resign and join me properly in this business? I have more and more orders and as things are, I have to get a manager. Why hire a manager when you can do the work better? What you earn in a month I earn in a day, working hard of course. But as our teachers told us in school, hard work never kills anybody. Please give it a serious thought, Chris. Our children are growing. We have to educate them, and we need all the resources both of us can pull together to do so.'

Chris thought it was a good idea, but what bothered him so much was having to work for his own wife. That was the way he thought about his wife's proposal, and that was the way all his colleagues, friends and relatives would think of Dora's proposal. It was unmanly to do that. He would not do it. He was the breadwinner and his wife was not going to feed him. Let her go on with her business. He owned her. Her property was his because she was his wife.

Dora seemed to have read Chris' mind and brought up the proposal again. 'Chris, it is a partnership. You will be the Managing Director and everything. I will do the donkey work. I need someone I trust to keep the books and to have an eye on everything. Please see with me.' But Chris did not see with her. He had other plans. He had other thoughts. He would go abroad and read law, return and be a lawyer. He was going to set up a lucrative practice when he returned. If he couldn't set up a practice, he would find a job in the civil service and continue taking . . .

By January of 1964, Chris completed the house in his home, and had it formally opened. Dora played down her part in the building of the house, and Chris took all the credit. In January of 1965, Chris was asked to transfer to Enugu. That was too much. He worked in Enugu for two years after leaving school, and thereafter was transferred to Ikot Ekpene. He had been there ever since. Why had they remembered him now? What post was he going to occupy in Enugu in 1965 when the political climate in the country was not certain? If he was still bent on going to England to read law, this was the time. He must leave the service now.

So he went to Enugu, saw people at the Head Office, and told them he wanted to be given a leave of absence without pay. The boss dealing with his case was relieved. He was being asked to transfer to Enugu as a punitive measure for all the misdemeanour reported against him. So he recommended that Chris be given three years study leave without pay.

Dora almost passed out when she heard the news from Chris. 'Three years Chris – you took the decision all alone? You did not ask my opinion? And the children? Am I to bring them up all by myself?' she wept.

'You can come along after six months; or you can leave the children with your mother and come.'

'And the business? Leave that with my mother as well? I have never heard such an irresponsible thing in all my life. Leave five children with my mother? You cannot be serious.'

'I am serious. Do you want me to end up in jail?'

'In jail?' Dora asked. Her anger had now given way to fear. 'Jail? I don't get it, Chris.'

'The transfer was a punitive act. I had to quit before they got concrete charges against me. Not that what I did was out

70

of the ordinary, everybody does it and gets away with it.'

'You have been taking bribes. You didn't have to do it.'

'How do you think I paid for the presents I sent you while you were in school?'

'Chris, all the Christian teachings in the Grammar School, didn't they influence you in any way? Oh, my God. And I thought I knew you, I . . .'

'We don't have much time now, I have to prepare to go abroad. I have to travel to Lagos for my passport, buy my ticket for M.V. Accra. Don't worry it will be all right.'

Dora was left at Ikot Ekpene with five small children, the eldest was only eleven. Chris arrived in London and enrolled in Gray's Inn. In three years he thought, he would be a lawyer. But he was not brilliant at school. He made a grade two all right, but he had not read for a long time. He had to start all over again, and after that job, a wife and five children, he could not have the peace of mind to take on law studies in London.

Dora worked hard as usual. Chris wrote letters, and after the first six months of his arrival in London, he stopped writing to Dora and the children. A year passed, the January 1966 coup met Dora at Ikot Ekpene. Things began to happen quickly, Dora was not deceived. A coup? There must be a counter one. What was she to do? The drama was being played out in Lagos and Kaduna no doubt, but Dora had the foresight that soon the world she used to know would change beyond recognition.

The first step she took, so as to counteract the sudden change that would inevitably come was to move her headquarters to Aba. It surprised her that she had not thought about it earlier. But then how could she, when Chris was working at Ikot Ekpene, and Aba was just an hour away by road. She found a good flat and moved her children. Her first daughter was already in Union Secondary School at Ibiaku. So she was left there, and she and the little ones settled in Aba. Her driver who was manager and store-keeper as well, got her a 'brother' to be in Ikot Ekpene. She

71

needed another van, but she did not want to purchase it just yet. She could wait. Dora did not see the reason for jubilation over the coup. Were those who were spared not guilty of bribes and corruption? Her teachers were right, independence came too soon. We had power thrust into our hands and we did not know what to do with it. We failed to use it judiciously. We became intolerant of those who opposed us; our political opponents became our enemies, and when they defeated us, we would not take defeat; we said the elections had been rigged. When a political party lost, overnight, its loss became victory, for during the dead of night, those who lost had bribed those who won, and a defeat turned to victory.

When Dora settled in Aba, the first thing she did was travel to Onitsha to put the house in order. But before she went, she thought she should look for the deed of lease. She remembered asking Chris about it but was not sure what his reply was.

She could not find the deed. She looked among all Chris' papers, it was not there. She became apprehensive. For the first time in her life she went to see a lawyer. When she finished, the lawyer told her that unless she could produce the deed nothing could be done. She was advised to go home to Onitsha and see the house all the same.

When Dora got to the house, a family was occupying it. Maybe Chris got tenants before he left for England. But why did he not tell her? She knew how much he took from the account. Why, what was going on? It was later on that she learnt that the house was not only rented out, but sold outright.

Dora returned from home exhausted, angry and sad. She went to the lawyer, told him what she found out, and was told that there was nothing she could do. Did she at any time sign a document? She did not. What then? An intelligent lady like her should know better, the elderly lawyer admonished. Dora bowed her head and wept. When she got home, the counter-coup had been announced, her children told her that the army had come again. 'Mama, they have come again,' the youngest child said. 'Mama, they have killed that big man, the Supreme Commander. They have killed him. They say they do not know where he is, but I know, they have killed him,' he went on.

'Keep quiet,' shouted Dora. She did not mean to shout, and she never shouted at her children, never. She was always very gentle with them. She was loving but firm. She was busy baking her bread and cake, but she found time to be with her children. She loved them, all five of them. But their father had betrayed her. He was a traitor. Why did Chris behave in the way he did? Why did he not tell her that he sold the house? Whoever sold a property in order to find the money to go abroad and study? Those who studied abroad returned home and bought land and built homes. Why sell the one you have in order to study abroad? It did not make any sense to her. She believed in him. She believed so much in Chris and now he had betrayed her.

She had a duty, and that duty was to her children. No matter what happened, she must give her children a good education. They would not be like her. They must go to the university like Agnes. Yes like Agnes. She heard about Agnes' success through Rose. Agnes had had her children and had gone to the university. Agnes was her own mistress now. Agnes could do what she liked, and there was no one on earth going to stop her.

The next morning Dora came to the conclusion that she had to go to England, if only to confront Chris and tell him that he was a let down. But how could she go? The army had taken over, it was not easy for anybody to move about in the country. She had to wait until the situation in the country settled, and pray that there will not be a civil war. God forbid that there should be a civil war. She read about the civil war in her history lessons – the American Civil War. Civil war was cruel. It was worse than any other type of war. God, she prayed, prevent us from having a civil war.

Dora had foresight. Even in July of 1966, she thought of

what to do. She had taken the first step towards survival by transferring her headquarters from Ikot Ekpene to Aba. The second step was to go to Onitsha, her husband's home. But their house had been sold, and therefore she must go to her own home which was a small obscure village in Orlu called Okporo.

So to Orlu she went. The only relative she had was her mother's sister whom she told to buy a piece of land for her, anything to take a small bungalow of four bedrooms. Her mother's sister had objected. 'Why, why are you spending valuable money buying land in Okporo? What are you going to do with it?'

'Build on it,' she had said impatiently. 'Get it for me at any cost.'

Before war was declared on July of 1967, Dora had completed her four-roomed bungalow. When the war was declared, she had furnished it and began to stock it with food. When Biafra over-ran the mid-west, she evacuated all her baking equipment from Aba, and set up her bakery in Okporo. She continued to work hard until Port Harcourt was evacuated and she could not find flour for her bakery. But then the World Council of Churches and the Caritas supplied her with flour, and she continued to bake in a 'win the war' oven. Her bakeries were still good. She had started making dry pack out of green plantains which she sent to the fighting soldiers in the Front. She even supplied Government House, Umuahia, when their supplies were delayed in Lisbon.

Dora got into contact with numerous refugees, especially from Onitsha, through her Eating Houses. And it was from one of them that she learnt who bought their house in Onitsha. She used all the resources she could muster, and since she was well to-do, and was self-sufficient when many people had lost their homes, she bought back her house, paid with Biafran currency and had the lease in her possession. In those days Biafran currency was not worth much, and there were people who carried it about in cartons and in the boot of their cars, but there were many others who did not have up to five hundred of it in their pockets.

But Dora had the money, and if the war meant having her home back, then the war could continue. Once Dora was able to do this, she began to look out for those in need who could part with the deeds of their property which were in 'enemy' hands. She was able to make two deals of this nature, one in Port Harcourt and the other in Aba.

So due to Dora's foresight, she and her family did not suffer too much during the civil war. She thought of her husband and wondered how he was. There was no way of contacting him. He had stopped writing to her even before war was declared. For she believed that he would return, if not for her sake, for the sake of the children. A man could abandon his wife, but not his children.

So when the war ended in January 1970, Dora came out of it, with her five children, and lost not even a pin and regained her house and two property deeds into the bargain. She went back to Aba to resume her business. People envied her. What kind of woman was Dora who was able to resume business soon after the war ended? What was she doing during the war? She must have been a saboteur to be able to organise herself so quickly. Dora heard all these murmurings, but never gave them a thought. She changed the Biafran notes she had for what they were worth in 'Nigerian' currency and turned her back to the war, and looked to the future. It was only in this way that she would be able to face life again.

Six months passed and when she heard nothing from her husband, she started making enquiries about him. She spoke to her husband's relations. There was nothing to hide any more. Hitherto, she had pretended, as if everything was all right. She had told her husband's relatives that Chris wrote to her regularly. Even during the war, she had kept on lying to them. Again her children had started asking embarrassing questions. 'Mother when will our father return from England? The war is now over. You said he could not return because of the war.'

'He will return,' Dora told them.

'But why doesn't he write to us? We want to write to him, mother,' said the youngest who did not know his father.

At eighteen, Dora's first daughter, Chinwe, was reluctant to go back to school. Dora put her foot down. 'You must go back to school. I don't want to hear that some of your school friends have gone to Lagos to look for jobs. You are not going to Lagos. You just have to get back to Union Secondary School, Ibiaku, where you were when the war started. Some of your friends will be there. And you have to start where the teachers say you will start. Yes three years have passed. You have lost those three years, but your education must be continued.'

Reluctantly, Chinwe returned to school. A year afterwards, she told her mother that she was through with school. She was more interested in doing business with her. She was so adamant about it that Dora let her stay. A year later, she got married to a businessman. She was only twenty.

Chinwe proved to be her mother's daughter. She was as industrious as her mother, and she not only baked, she also went into full catering business. Her husband did importing and exporting business, and in no time at all they were both well off.

In 1974, Chinwe decided to go to London ostensibly to have a check up which was becoming fashionable at the time. She went to the address of her father's when they last heard from him, but was told that there was nobody bearing that name. In fact no Nigerian had lived there for the past five years.

Dora took the news calmly. Before Chinwe finished her story, she decided on what to do. She would go to London herself. Of course she knew someone in Lagos. Agnes lived in Lagos. She would be of use to her. She would stay with her. Then make inquiries from Chris' relatives in Lagos. She knew a relative who was sympathetic to her during the war. He must know Chris' whereabouts.

Agnes was living to Ikoyi and had a very good job. It was

easy for Dora to locate her, and with her help Chris' relative was found. An address was given to Dora, and she flew to London, armed with the address. Yes, someone knew about Chris there. Chris was very much involved with the Biafan war, and when it ended, he went to Germany.

So Dora took the next plane to Hamburg armed with the address she was given. She arrived at the flat and rang the bell. A sleepy German lady opened the door, saw Dora and shut the door again. Dora waited for what she thought was the longest ten minutes in all her life. Then the door opened, and Chris, in a dressing gown, walked out of the flat, put his hands in his pockets and asked Dora what she wanted. Dora stared back at him, 'Papa . . .' She stopped. Perhaps she had made a mistake. She looked at the man who was standing before her. No, she had made a mistake. The man who stood before her was bald. Chris' hair was full before he left home for England. She was no longer sure. The man waited and said not a word. Dora opened her handbag and brought out the address and gave it to the man. He did not take it. He asked again, 'What do you want?' she recognised the voice. It was Chris who was standing in front of her. It was Chris who pretended that he did not know her. It was Chris, her childhood love, her husband, the father of her children.

'Chris, it is Dora.'

'I know it is Dora all right. What do you want?'

'I want you, Chris, I want . . .'

The door opened again and the German lady who opened it at first walked out and said something in German. She opened the door again, went in and banged the door. 'I am afraid you have to go back to the airport. All I can do for you is phone a taxi which will take you to the airport. Here is not Nigeria. People don't just visit without notice.'

'But Chris, I wrote you, I . . .'

'You did, but I did not say come. You should have waited to hear from me.'

'Chris, I have waited these years, the children, the war, everything . . .'

Dora stopped as she heard Chris phoning then she heard him coming back, it was a long corridor, and flats were on either side of it. She was tired, she felt ill, was it dizziness or what. 'God let me not faint. God don't allow me to faint. Please God. Please God.' She neither heard nor saw Chris. She was aware that she was in a taxi. She didn't speak that language, so she said nothing to the taxi driver. Then she saw the airport, the taxi stopped, the driver brought down her only suitcase and said something. She brought out the money she had; and gave it to the taxi driver. He took it, and gave her some change which she took, and went inside the airport. There was the information desk. Lufthansa will be flying to London in two hours. She checked in and waited for the plane.

The next day, she took another plane to Lagos, then to Aba. For a week she stayed in her bedroom. She looked at herself in the mirror. She was not bad. Then she removed all her clothes and looked in the mirror again. She was not bad. She ran both hands over her head. Yes, she still had long hair. She had not lost any hair. She looked young. At least Chris aged. She hadn't aged. That must be a consolation. What happened to Chris in London and Hamburg? What went wrong with Chris? Her sympathy dramatically turned to Chris. At first she had locked herself up and felt sorry for herself. Now she felt sorry for Chris. He should not have gone to England in the first place. She told him, but he did not listen to her. And the German lady? Was she Chris' 'wife' or concubine or what? Was she keeping Chris? When did Chris go to Hamburg? Why Hamburg? No, she must stop all these questions which had no answers. She must do˙something. But what? What was she going to do?

A month after her return from London and Hamburg, she went to Chris' home, got hold of his old relatives and divorced him by native law and custom. A few days afterwards, Tunde came into her life.

Chapter 6

Rose

At Queen's College Lagos, Rose attempted the entrance to the University College, Ibadan and failed. She returned home to Aba, taught in a girls school and attempted the entrance to Ibadan again and passed. She was admitted into Ibadan in 1953, and missed Ernest who had left Ibadan and gone abroad to continue his medical studies.

Ibadan days passed quickly for Rose. She graduated and went to the University of London for her Diploma in Education. While in London she tried to find Ernest, but could not. She returned to Nigeria and was appointed as Woman Education Officer in Queen's College, where she taught maths.

It was at the latter part of 1958 that Rose met Mark. He was one of the most brilliant men Rose had ever met. He had already passed his B.Sc Maths as a private student and had the ambition of going to the United States of America to read economics. While Mark worked in the Ministry of Labour, he applied to be admitted to Harvard or Yale.

Mark meant a lot to Rose. In Ibadan, she worked hard, danced, attended parties and passed her exams making good grades. But she was not attached to any person. The kind of relationship she now had with Mark was new and fresh. Nothing like that had happened to her before.

One day Mark visited her at her flat in Onikan. They had supper and listened to music. It was getting late, but Mark made no attempt to leave. When it was eleven he said, matter of factly, that he would spend the night. So he spent the night with Rose for the first time, and afterwards stayed with Rose.

What intrigued Rose so much was Mark's domesticity, He took over the cooking. He cleaned the house and he even baked. Rose was taught all these chores at home and ACMGS all right, but she did not particularly enjoy doing them. She ate once a day, and bought her cakes from a Ghanaian woman down the street who made beautiful cakes.

So Rose started thinking of Mark seriously. Suddenly, Lagos changed for her. Mark took her to interesting places. She returned home from work to see that Mark was already home. Rose no longer said, 'I want to do this, or I shall do that,' but 'we want to go to the pictures,' or 'what are we going to do tonight?'

Then one night, Mark proposed to Rose and she accepted. It happened in a most dramatic way. She and Mark were having supper one evening when one of Mark's friends walked in. Rose knew him by name but had never seen him. He joined them and after the meal, he and Mark went out. Mark did not return until after midnight, and Rose could not sleep because she had to sit up waiting for him.

'I hope there is nothing wrong,' Rose said as she opened the door for Mark.

'Nothing at all. John has a problem with his wife,' he said and began to remove all his clothes.

'You did not tell me John was married,' said Rose innocently.

'Oh, John has a woman living with him, just . . .' He stopped. Had he gone bananas? Was was wrong with him?

'Come on darling let's go to bed. It's late and you have a long day tomorrow, or rather, this morning.' Mark lifted her up and kissed her, put her down, and started removing her nightdress. Then he carried her again to the bed, and proposed to her and she accepted, and then they made love.

Mark talked Rose into applying for scholarship, or taking leave of absence to do a doctorate degree in Mathematics in Harvard or Yale. He said it was a pity that such a brain as

Rose's would be utilised only in teaching maths to girls in Queen's College. Rose thought it was a good idea, and she began to think of it seriously. It was at this stage that Mark told her that he had been admitted to Harvard, and had been asked to make a deposit so that his place would be kept for him before he got his passport. He also gave Rose some forms to fill for her own admission. Time was running out, therefore Mark decided to go home to Aba and speak to his father.

He returned two days before he was expected and told Rose that his father was in hospital at Anua, and he spent all the money he had to pay medical fees. He was too gentlemanly to ask Rose for a direct loan, but Rose understood. Since she would also come to Harvard she suggested that they got married before he left.

Mark said it was a good idea. He suggested that Rose, after marriage, should keep her maiden name, so that the Ministry of Education would find it easier to give her a leave of absence. Rose agreed. The wedding was to be very simple. Mark did not like noise of any kind. Marriage was just for two people. Why the noise and fanfare? So the date was fixed and Rose and Mark came to the Registry in Lagos from their work places. One of the clerks was their witness. And after the ceremony they went back to work.

They spent a glorious one week honeymoon in Rose's flat, and soon it was time for Mark to travel to the States. But he did not have enough money to buy his air ticket and even pay his fees. So Rose withdrew all her savings, and handed it over to him. He thanked her. It would be all right as soon as he got to Harvard. He would work. He had a relative who would support him. By the time Rose came, he would be on his own, and would in turn look after his wife.

So Rose sent a letter to the Principal which was drafted by Mark himself to say that she was married, but that she preferred to be referred to and called by her maiden name. This was a bit odd, but since it was Rose's wish, the Principal complied and wrote to the Federal Ministry of Education so as to keep the records straight. A few days afterwards, a reply was sent to the Principal saying that since Rose was married she must go by her married name, otherwise she would be treated officially as a single woman. For some reason Rose did not inform Mark of this letter, but asked the principal to say that she preferred to be treated as a single woman officially. And there the matter rested.

With the help of Mark, Rose got her passport, withdrew all her savings and gave it to Mark. She was to follow him as soon as she was admitted into Harvard. Mark wrote a week after his arrival in the States, and said he would write again as soon as he settled down, and had an address. But weeks, months passed and Rose did not hear from Mark. She was not acquainted as such with Mark's friends, so she could not ask them about Mark. She even wondered whether Mark told his friends especially John that they were married.

She took a leave of absence and visited Aba where Mark said his parents were, but his parents were not there. She came back to Lagos. Slowly it began to dawn on her that Mark had jilted her. She had lost contact with Ernest, now Mark. She was miserable. She felt sorry for herself. She wept, but she shared her sorrow with no one. She went about her business with great effort but she controlled her emotions. Thank God she was not pregnant. But couldn't it have been better if she were pregnant? After all, her friends in ACMGS were married and had children. If she were pregnant, she would have had something to look forward to, a baby, boy or girl it did not matter. Nearly eight years after leaving school, she could only boast of a degree and nothing else. But she consoled herself. Mark was not the end of the world. To forget and look forward to the future, Rose decided to leave Queen's and look for another job in Lagos. Of course where else? So in 1959 she got a job with a firm of Public Relations.

Rose worked hard and in eighteen months, she had become a high executive. She was sent abroad for training for only three weeks, and she returned full of new ideas and vigour. Independence was round the corner. Nigerians were being trained to take over from the British. Rose was lucky to be in a position where she would use her brain and talent, and so she used it well.

She regretted the time she wasted in Queen's. But then as we say, any time you wake up is your morning. She was where she was at the right time. She moved to Ikoyi, had a large office and a secretary. If that was not success, what then was success? She thought of her school, her lovely and caring teachers, and the Christian upbringing she had had. At other times she thought of Ernest. Where was he? Why did she succumb to Mark? How on earth did Mark succeed in tricking her and depriving her of her good name and her life savings? But again, like Dora, she had to look to the future and turn her back on the past. In so doing, she would make a success of her life again.

She kept in touch with Dora. She wrote her occasionally, and she saw Agnes from time to time. Rose was in her office one day when her secretary, Tinu told her that someone who called herself Janet wanted to see her. 'Janet?' Rose asked. 'Yes, Janet' Tinu replied. 'Ask her to come in.'

Janet came into the office. Rose stared at the woman who called herself Janet, and pressed the bell. Tinu came in. She looked at her, and looked at the woman. Tinu had the piece of paper in which Janet wrote her name, and showed it to her boss. Rose could not reconcile the handwriting and the woman in front of her. Rose did what they used to do in those good old days, she went forward to embrace Janet. Janet stretched out both hands, 'Don't touch me. Nobody touches me on a Friday.'

Rose's secretary opened the door quietly and left. Rose looked at Janet. Her dress was torn at the sides. It was dirty, old and shapeless. Her headtie was a dirty rag which carefully covered her beautiful hair completely. She kept pulling at the headtie, as she talked with Rose. She wore a pair of brown sandals, and a bandage or a rag was tied on the ankle of her left leg. The sore smelt as if it had not been washed for days. It looked as if it had been there for years. Rose found no words. Janet sat on the chair in front of her desk.

'Janet, welcome to Lagos, when did you come?' said Rose at last. Janet said nothing. It was Janet all right. Rose did not make a mistake. She sat there admiring the office. Rose tried again: 'Janet, welcome to my office. Today does not happen to be Friday, today is Tuesday. However what can I do for you? Can I get you some coffee?'

She shook her head vigorously. Then she opened her dirty handbag, got a pill and put it into her mouth, then she said, 'Rose, please ask your secretary to give me a glass of cold water.' When the water was brought, she got another pill, popped it into her mouth, and drank the water with relish.

'Do you want something to eat? My secretary can get us some sandwiches next door,' said Rose.

'No thank you, I don't eat sandwiches on Friday,' said Janet.

'But Janet, today is Tuesday, not Friday. You must eat something, before you tell me why you have come to see me. I can see you have eaten nothing for days. Please eat something.'

Janet refused to eat the sandwiches when they were brought. Then, after Rose persuaded her to tell her why she had come, she told Rose that she wanted a job and that she was told that only Rose could give her a job. Again she wanted Rose to get in touch with her husband so that he would release her children from jail. She said she was not insane at all but her husband and his relatives had told everybody that she was mad. Rose agreed to help her, and she left.

It was several weeks after this visit that Rose met Comfort at the Levantis Stores in Marina. Comfort looked well. Time did not tell too much on her. She was as vivacious as ever. After her school certificate exam, she trained for a little while at Aba, and before the year was out went abroad and qualified in Nursing and Midwifery. At Middlesex Hospital she had met and married Dr. Oyele, and they had three children. Comfort was not working as a nurse any more. She said it was not really her profession, she wanted to teach, but when she asked her husband to let her go abroad and do the Tutors Course in nursing, he refused. So she stayed at home looking after her husband and children and doing some contract work with the Ministry of Works.

Rose told her about Janet's visit to her office. 'You remember that night Janet sharpened a matchet to kill me? Whatever was wrong started at that time. She has not been stable. She had to be confined in an institution, but sometimes, she escapes from confinement. She must have gone back by now,' said Comfort, who knew the story of nearly everybody who passed through ACMGS especially her class mates. Rose was sad about Janet, but she thanked God for His mercies. Why should she worry so much because she was single when Janet was in an institution?

Rose kept in touch with her friends. She wrote to Dora after Janet's visit. Dora wrote back telling her all her problems and how she was trying to cope with them. She referred to Rose's problems as well and told her that one day God would reward her with a good man. Soon after this letter, Olu entered Rose's life.

Olu had come to do business in Rose's office. It was a matter which Tinu could have handled very well. But for one reason or the other, Tinu asked her boss to see Olu. He was in Rose's office for exactly thirty minutes. Tinu served him a special coffee reserved for VIPs. He drank it slowly while they discussed the problem. He asked for another cup, and commented that it was very good coffee. Rose saw him to the door after the discussion, and it was there he asked Rose whether she would have lunch with him the next day.

Rose had no lunch appointment, so she accepted. Olu said he would send his driver to collect Rose at one thirty. Promptly, at one thirty the driver was announced. Rose dashed to the toilet, looked at herself in the mirror, applied lipstick and dashed out again. 'See you Tinu,' she said. Tinu

85

called her back, adjusted the collar of her dress, and asked if she should wait for her to return. Rose asked her to wait. While in the car, she wondered why Tinu asked that question. She always came back to the office any time clients took her to lunch.

The driver took unfamiliar streets and within fifteen minutes they were in Victoria Island, then the driver stopped at a block of flats and they went up in the lift. It was a beautiful flat, tastefully furnished. A steward ushered Rose in and asked what she would like to drink. Then Olu came out from one of the rooms, and shook hands with Rose, then asked her over to the table.

Lunch was 'eba' and 'amala' with okra and 'ewedu' stew. Olu opened the wine himself and served Rose. They talked as they ate. Olu was a businessman who did big business. He came to Rose's office to talk about a small business he was setting up for his wife, and he had wanted the firm to do some studies for him. He had offices in London and New York, and beautiful homes as well. He told Rose he loved his food, and whenever he travelled, and he travelled fairly often, he took his food with him. To him the greatest barriers in the world between different cultures were not just language but food. He paid a fortune to entertain his business associates in hotels in London and New York, but he returned to his flat afterwards to eat aba with okra egusi or ewedu soup.

Olu was accomplished. He was interested in the arts. He discussed Nigerian writers, dramatists and artists. For a Nigerian tycoon to discuss in that way, he was really educated. He won Rose's admiration immediately, but she had to be careful, after Mark.

However her whole life changed, she and Olu went out together after that lunch. Olu was eager to talk about himself. He had inherited some landed property from his mother, and he was an only child. But his father had other children by other women, and when he died, the children began to quarrel amongst themselves over property. Olu was

86

the eldest. He brought everybody together, and the dispute was amicably settled.

He was thirty then and unmarried. It did not surprise anyone when he returned to Lagos, two years afterwards with a black American girl and two sons. The American girl preferred to live in New York instead of Lagos.

Rose saw herself thinking of Olu. She tried not to be too involved, she tried not to be emotional, but it was difficult. She had to learn this. She must learn. She must be like Comfort who sailed in from one relationship to the other without being the worse for it.

Rose started thinking of a one parent family. Agnes and Dora were right when they told her that she could get involved with a man, be pregnant and be the mother of his child. Why should she not relax and be pregnant? Rose confided in her secretary, Tinu, who was happy about it, and covered Rose's path very well. Then she talked to an experienced midwife, who told Rose what to do. She did it, but nothing happened. Then she said to hell with pregnancy. She was having the most wonderful time of her life. She decided to relax and make the best out if it while it lasted. Why not? Olu was giving her all those things she thought Ernest would give her, but did not. Mark exploited her. She kept him and he jilted her. Olu was there, he was good to her and he took care of her emotional problems. He did not keep her. He did not buy her expensive gifts, so she did not feel indebted to him in any way. But she loved to be with him.

One day Olu came to Rose's office and asked her whether she could afford two weeks holiday in London. She could. She was her own boss, so she could take a holiday conveniently. Olu sent the return ticket through the driver whom Rose gave five pounds tip. The driver pocketed the money and thanked her respectfully. The return ticket read, Lagos – London – Paris – London – Lagos. They took different air-lines and arrived at the hotel on the same day.

After a most wonderful one week stay in London, Olu received a call from New York and so had to go. While he was away, Rose discovered that she was pregnant. She spent the next days thinking. Rose kept asking herself, 'Should I tell him or should I not?' She decided not to tell him, and to go back to Lagos immediately. But she must at least inform him. She dialled his number in New York and Olu's wife answered. She dropped the telephone.

She then dropped a note for Olu in his London office, shopped for two hours on Oxford Street and took the plane back to Lagos, to her home, and her office which was her sanctuary. Tinu was surprised to see her boss. She welcomed her and followed her to her office. Then she told her. She was happy for her. Tinu arranged for a midwife to see Rose. There was something about her which Rose did not like. However, she told her what she must not do – no sex, no spirits of any kind, no coffee, no tea, nothing hot at all, only cold water.

Rose tried not to worry. She hadn't heard from Olu, and there was no way of reaching him. She talked to her secretary a good deal. She encouraged her and Rose kept her fingers crossed. She did not mind a boy or a girl. Any baby was welcome provided it was a normal baby. Rose prayed that God should not give her an abnormal baby.

At four months, Rose felt the baby in her womb. She prayed, she rested. Then one day while she was in the office working Tinu rushed into her room saying 'Madam, hide, hide in the toilet, quick . . .' Before she had time to think of what she said, she acted instinctively and dashed into the toilet and bolted the door. Fear gripped her. What was the matter? Why was she hiding? Then she heard Tinu say distinctly, 'Madam is not in. She did not come to work today . . .'

'Don't give me that garbage. Her car is at the car park. I want to see her. I want to warn her to steer clear of my husband or . . .'

'Just what are you talking about? Who is your husband? This is the office of Mrs Wilson, you are in the wrong room. I am sorry, Madam . . .' Tinu tried to steer her to the door for she was in Rose's office, and Rose heard everything. 'I have heard about you. Warn her. If she does not leave my husband alone, I'll kill her, by Jove, I'll kill her. And . . .'

Tinu pushed her out and shut the door, 'Now you get out of this building before I call the security officer. Do you want to leave or do you want to be carried out from this building?' Olu's wife stood her ground. She was a small woman, but she looked quite strong. She returned 'fire for fire' until the security officer forcibly carried her out of the building, but she made sure she scratched his face with her long nails.

Rose stayed in the toilet for about five minutes before Tinu knocked and told her that it was safe outside. She took her down through the Emergency Exit to the carpark and drove Rose in her own car to her home. She asked Rose's maid to cook, and after the meal which Rose could not eat, she gave her two tablets of phenobarb, remained with her until six o'clock, then she went home.

The next morning, Rose menstruated for the first time in five months.

Rose never saw Olu again. She threw herself into her work. She went for another course overseas and came back just about the time the country was restive as a result of the elections of 1964, and as usual, the foreigners were better informed of what was going on than the nationals, so they took precautions. Rose, like all other Nigerians at the time, did not see why the foreigners too should be apprehensive. Their apprehension dawned on Rose when, on returning from Ibadan one afternoon, she witnessed the burning of three cars at the Yaba roundabout. She had never been so frightened in all her life. She saw the thugs terrorise the drivers and the occupants of the cars. She saw the occupants running away for dear life. The thugs opened the tanks of the cars and threw in lighted matches. The cars were set ablaze; while the thugs entered their van and escaped.

When she narrated the incident to her boss, she was told that she was lucky the thugs did not burn her car as well. 'But I am not a politician,' she cried.

'No, you are not. But the man they burnt to death at Agege a few weeks ago was not a politician. His was a case of mistaken identity,' said her boss. 'That's why we must be very careful. We have to watch events as closely as possible.'

All that Miss Hill had told them when they were in school was coming true. No, Nigeria was not ready for independence. Nigeria needed time to mature, to be a nation. Nigeria needed time to learn that when they were independent, it did not just mean taking over from the colonial masters. It meant taking over responsibility from the colonial masters. It meant being patriotic, taking decisions that would benefit the country just as the colonial masters took decisions that benefited the mother country.

For Rose, the future of Nigeria was bleak. With so much violence going on, how could the country survive? Things were not getting better when a political party boycotted the elections by not only making a statement but causing the election booths to be destroyed. Political opponents were being burnt alive in their homes and on the streets. And the question on everybody's lips at the time was whether Nigeria would survive as a nation.

It was in the midst of all these uncertainties in the country that Ernest appeared again into Rose's life. Rose was rather busy in the office one morning when Tinu told her that there was a man who called himself Ernest who wanted to see her urgently. 'Ask him to come in,' Rose simply said. Ernest came in and he was in fact Ernest. Time had not changed his looks much. But it had changed his thinking a good deal as Rose could see later. She wondered why he had come to see her after such a long time. They shook hands and she asked him to sit down, while Tinu made him coffee. He drank his coffee quietly but said nothing. 'Perhaps you want to talk and the office isn't the right place,' said Rose for want of any other thing to say.

'I would have come to your home, but I hesitated. I wasn't sure whether you would be disposed to see me. Now I am sure. But perhaps it would be a good idea if we talked at home. I only returned from London two days ago. I hope to go home, see my mother and go back again. I have one or two things to settle before I finally return home. You have not changed much Rose.' Rose said nothing. But they agreed that he should visit Rose in her house that evening at seven o'clock.

The rest of the day passed quickly. Rose was a bit agitated at seeing Ernest and at his impending visit. What did he want to say to her after all these years? She had heard from Comfort that Ernest was involved with an Irish girl in Dublin. The rest of the story she did not want to hear let alone find out whether it was true. She had felt disappointed at the way Ernest faded out of her life after all the affectionate letters at school and Yaba. It was Ernest who ignored all her letters and so she stopped writing. Now Ernest had come, and wanted to see her.

Rose's sitting room was tastefully furnished. The chairs were small but elegant. At the centre of the room was a beautiful Persian rug, and a delicate oblong table. The rest of the floor was bare, but very well polished, so well polished that one could almost see one's face on the floor. At the right hand corner was the television and a small transistor radio. At the other end was a side table and a bowl of fresh flowers.

Ernest took in the whole place all at once, picked a chair and sat down crossing his legs. 'What would you like to drink?' Rose asked.

'Just beer, and make it the small bottle, Star preferably.' Rose brought him that, and poured herself a sherry. 'You live in beautiful surroundings,' said Ernest.

'Thank you. The house belongs to the company. I am only a tenant.'

'Of course I know that. I meant the inside. You have good taste. Won't you show me the rest of the house?'

'Later,' she said and went to the kitchen, came out and told him that dinner was served.

As they were eating, Ernest began to talk of old times. Where were Dora, Agnes and Comfort? He did not have the

91

pleasure of knowing them well, but Rose always mentioned them in her letters. 'Do you remember those letters we used to write to each other?' asked Ernest. Rose remembered but since she was determined to forget the past and look to the future, she told Ernest that she did not remember. He sensed of course that she did not want to talk about old times.

They ate, almost without relish, then Ernest began to talk: 'You must forgive my awkwardness Rose. I have come to see you to make my apologies and to ask for forgiveness. Then, I can make my proposal. I felt that I must make my confession in person, and I don't want to know whether it is too late or not. I received all your letters. I had a great problem at the time. I was doing well in my school, when during the holidays, I was invited to Dublin by a friend who studied there. We went out to dance on the third day of my stay in Dublin. There I met an Irish girl who danced so well. We danced and we drank, I must have been drunk. My friend took his own girl with him when the dance ended, and I took mine with me. After what seemed to be a pleasant and relaxing one week in Dublin, I went back to London.

'Three months later, I received a letter from this girl, I must confess, I did not know her name, saying that she was pregnant. What was I to do? By the time I recovered from the shock of this girl's letter I received another one from her mother saying that she was going to report to the police if her daughter aborted the pregnancy. I was afraid. I contacted my friend in Dublin, but he did not give me any useful suggestions. "You should have been careful, after all, you are a medical student. You knew the implications of what you were doing."

'By the end of the second week, my professor called me and handed me a letter from the girl's mother. I was shattered . . .' Rose had stopped eating now, and listened attentively. When she saw that Ernest had finished his beer, she went to the kitchen and brought another, opened it and poured it into Ernest's glass. 'That was the last straw,' continued Ernest. "I guess I have to marry her," I said to my professor. He said nothing. To cut a long story short Rose, I got myself a "wife" without being prepared to have one. I used to wonder in some quiet moments, if this girl was thrust upon me by those who did not like me. Was it all planned? Why was my friend not helpful when I wrote him? And why had he not written to console me or to sympathise? Why did he not warn me in the first place about Dublin and her girls? Was it fair for me or the girl to be man and wife just because of this mistake?

'So we lived together. When she had her baby, it was a pure disaster. Neither she nor I was prepared for parenthood. I was almost crazy. I had failed my examinations twice, and there was talk that I would be asked to leave if I failed again. I did not want to do the examination again because if I did I would fail and so lose my place. So I told this girl that she had to find a job, and that we would have to get foster parents for our baby girl, and that I had to pass my examinations and go home to my people.

'It was then that she told me that she had left school at sixteen and worked in a grocery shop in Dublin. She did not want to work. She said she wanted to look after her daughter, and that she hated the idea of fostering her baby girl. I was at my wits' end. Did she not know that I could fail my examinations again if she did not comply to my suggestions? Did she not know that I had no money to keep her and the baby? She knew all right, as she told me, but she was not going to part with her first baby.

'Then I wrote to her mother asking her to come and talk sense into her daughter. She replied to say that her daughter was married to me and she did not want to interfere. It was my duty to talk to her and if she liked, she could do as I wished her to do. I wrote back suggesting that she should come to London, and help me settle the problem. She demanded a return fare and an allowance per day while she stayed with us.

'In the midst of all these problems, I received a message from home saying that my father had died suddenly. I clutched the letter as if someone was going to snatch it from me. I walked in the park talking to myself until a policeman came, tapped me on the shoulder and told me it was time to go home. I told him I was finished, that my father had died suddenly, and that my young wife had a baby, and I was in no shape to take control of myself. I gave him my address, and he walked me home, and told me that a man who could not face his problems was not a man. Just as he was about to leave, my baby cried, and my wife came out carrying her in her arms, perhaps to get her something to eat. The policeman stared at her in disbelief. He bowed, and touched his cap, my wife blushed, went to the kitchen and remained there until the policeman left.

'Soon after, I heard from my mother. My father's relatives had started to molest her. They remembered the insults heaped upon them by my mother when my father was alive. They accused my mother of even being responsible for the death of my father. They made life thoroughly difficult for her while she mourned my father.

'I was heart-broken when I read the letter. Of course my allowances stopped immediately. My father was not a rich man as such, but he was not a poor man either. He sent me to England, he had a good job. The United Africa Company (UAC) helped with my allowance in England while he paid them in Nigeria. When he died, the allowance stopped. So I had to stop studies entirely and got a job. A job in the factory! The more I worked, the less I had to feed the family. We had to move to a basement apartment, and it was very cold. The toilet was somewhere on the first floor of the flat. There was no bathroom. I could afford one bath a week in the public bath. My "wife" did not have one for several months. Sometimes, when I could not bear it any longer, I took her to the bath myself, and made sure she had a bath.

'Life was tough, Rose. That was not what the Irish girl bargained for. She had seen Nigerian students in Dublin and how they lived. Many of them owned cars, and were quite well off. So I was not surprised when I returned from work

94

one evening to see that she had run away, and left our girl in the pram. Till this day, I think that it was the policeman who made me realise for the first time that my "wife" was an attractive girl.

'Well,' Ernest went on, 'Nigerian neighbours who hitherto minded their own business rallied round. They found foster parents and my beautiful daughter was taken away by them. She was nearly a year old then. Rose, I will never see her again. She keeps haunting me. I may meet her in the street and we will be perfect strangers.'

The food was cold. Neither of them realised that they were not eating. The record had stopped playing. Long after Ernest had finished his tale, both were busy with their own thoughts. Rose wondered why Ernest had come and why he found it necessary to tell her all he had told her. Ernest wondered whether Rose understood the motive of his visit. Was she prepared to give him another chance? It was a long time, but he had Rose in mind all these years. His misfortune and sufferings were responsible for his inability to get in touch with his childhood sweetheart.

Rose got up first. She was the hostess after all. She cleared the table while Ernest sat down on the armchair. She brought some fruits, he declined and said he wanted more beer. She brought him another beer while she ate her pawpaw. Then she looked at her watch and saw that it was after five o'clock. 'I must drive you to your hotel,' she said. Ernest looked confused but said nothing. She dashed into the room, came out with the key of the car and asked him whether he was ready. He was ready, and they drove towards Surulere.

'Can I see you again tomorrow?' asked Ernest.

'You said you were going home to see your mother tomorrow,' said Rose.

'That can wait. I have not told you why I came to you. I have some proposals to make Rose, please don't put me off.'

'I am not putting you off. It is just that first things should be done first. See your mother, and when you come back to

Lagos you can call on me. We have a seminar this week, and I have not prepared the papers yet. I am organising it. And I hate to be found wanting.'

When they got to the hotel, Ernest thanked Rose and they agreed to meet when he returned from his mother.

He spent only two days with his mother and returned to Rose. 'As I said,' Ernest said to Rose. 'I have a proposal to make. I have been to see my mother, and now I can make the proposal. Please listen to me very carefully. I come to you with all humility and a sense of responsibility. I have talked to my mother and I want you to be my wife. Why I came to Nigeria was to see you and see my mother. I shall go back and return in eighteen months. Please don't say no.'

This baffled Rose. Their love had been childish. All they had done was exchange love letters written in blue writing pads with envelopes to match. During the holidays, they held hands and talked about their schools and what they would do when they left school, the high lights of their holiday enjoyment were going to the cinema, and very occasionally going to dance together with the brass band of the central school playing.

'This has taken me by surprise, Ernest. It is a long time and it is not easy to say yes or no. Go back to London, let's have an open mind about your proposal. I shall be here,' said Rose.

'Thank you. That's what I wanted to hear. I am glad. You will please look after my mother when I am gone,' and with this, he left. But before Ernest could return, the political situation in the country had worsened, giving rise to the January 15th coup of 1966, and the civil war in 1967. Rose was in Lagos and remained there until the end of the war in 1970.

Chapter 7

As soon as the war had ended, Rose went to the East. She saw her people and saw Dora in Aba. She was surprised that Dora was financially all right. She, unlike her people, did not need rehabilitation as such. But she had brought her a few things she knew she would need, like cosmetics and some pants and underwear. She was also glad that all her children came out of the war alive.

They decided to visit their old school, and used Dora's van. They were surprised at the devastation of their beautiful school. The chapel was no more, and what's more soldiers were quartered there. Rose could not imagine the kind of hardship suffered by the Biafrans. No matter how Dora tried to describe it, Rose could not understand. 'What bothered you most?' asked Rose, trying to understand.

'Air raids,' she said. 'But we were lucky, I mean my children and I. I saw what was coming in time, so I prepared for it. We did not suffer unduly. We suffered no hunger. I baked bread, cakes and other things.'

'We in Lagos felt for our brothers and sisters in Biafra. But there was nothing we could do. And since there was nothing I could do personally, I made it a habit to go to church every Sunday and pray for the war to end,' said Rose. 'And, Dora, it helped. I mean it helped me emotionally. I had that faith that one day it would end, and my family and friends would come out alive. And when you visited Lagos on your way to England, I did not see you,' continued Rose.

'No, you were not in Lagos. Your secretary said you went to Kaduna or Kano I don't know which. So I stayed with

Agnes. Never mind, it was just a few days' stay. And you know of course what happened to me in Germany.'

'You told me,' said Rose.

'Well, there is nothing to do now. It hurts Rose. Chris' behaviour was overwhelming. I had to develop a kind of courage to contain my anger and frustration. Heaven knows I bent over backwards to make the marriage work.'

'But Dora, you have Tunde now,' said Rose.

'Yet, but it is not the same. Having Tunde doesn't make the disappointment easier to bear. Well, what cannot be helped must be endured, and as they say in Ikot Ekpene "man no die i no rotten".'

Rose laughed aloud. 'Say that again.'

'Man no die i no rotten,' Dora repeated. 'There is a great philosophy in that saying,' continued Dora. 'Those people in Ikot Ekpene are wonderful. They are gentle and kind. Rather philosophical in their behaviour. They take life as it comes and never seem to be in too much hurry like our own people, who seem to be pursued by a thousand demons in their everyday activities. I had a good time there.'

'Man no die i no rotten,' Rose repeated.

'Listen to this,' said Dora. 'When you ask an Ikot Ekpene man how far Anua is, he will answer, "sometime one mile; sometime two mile".'

Rose roared with laughter. Then she said, 'And you had to leave Ikot Ekpene for Aba.'

'I had no choice. I had to go. Aba was so different. The people were over-dynamic and rough. But my business thrived. But Rose, business is not all that there is in life. One wants more in life. Little things that satisfy. Like good company, good films, and an occasional party with one's friends.'

'You didn't have those in Aba,' said Rose.

'Well, before the war no, but after the war, things began to change a bit. Some enlightened people came to Aba to live.'

'Why are you comparing then? and what about Tunde?' asked Rose.

Dora got up, shook her head vigorously as if she wanted to shake away her blues, and went gingerly to the kitchen. Rose followed her. She opened the refrigerator and found it was empty. 'I live here alone.' Rose read her like a book.

'You have kids to look after, I don't.'

'I can organise something fast for you. But what about beer, drink some beer, while I prepare some food.'

'I am not particularly hungry,' she said. 'Do you have some table-wine, not sweet but dry, not Mateus rosé, please.'

Rose had it and gave her good well chilled dry wine. 'You haven't told me much about Tunde. Your letters have been quite sketchy about him,' Rose said, pouring herself a glass of wine and sitting down.

'Tunde is nice,' she said. 'He is handsome, of average height, he is all that and more Dora, but you see . . .'

'See what?' Rose asked.

'It is not the same.'

'What is not the same?'

'A husband and a lover.'

'But you have a good business and you have your children, and now you have Tunde. I don't quite understand you, and . . . He is there, not always of course, but he is there. He helps you emotionally and perhaps financially. Though I am not married, I have always believed that it is better to marry and be divorced, than not marry at all; it is better to have a bad husband than none at all. Your case is even better. You have your children, you have your business and you have Tunde.'

'Rose, there is a great difference between a husband and a lover,' Dora insisted.

'Well, you should know, having had both. I have never had a husband, so I feel inadequate. But from what I have read in books and from experiences of other people, one should rather have a husband than a lover. There are so many advantages, I think. But can one combine a husband with a lover?'

'I am not certain that I can, Rose. Maybe people like Comfort and others in school with us can do so. I hear stories in Aba and Port Harcourt, but . . .'

'Well here in Lagos, it is the thing. Women with grown up children, who may or may not live with their husbands, have lovers. Some of these lovers are young enough to be their sons.'

'You mean it?' asked Dora in horror.

'I have no proof. It is said everywhere especially when you attend a party. I am told of cases where a husband and a wife meet each other at a party.

'And what happens?'

'This is Lagos. Both are civilised. They know what each does, so they take it well.'

'And they go back home, and live together?'

'Of course' said Rose.

'The world is coming to an end, then.'

'No, not yet. It is our brand of civilisation. Our society is rotten.'

'Our grandfathers will turn in their graves if they hear of the men who know of their wives' carrying on, and do nothing about it'.

'When the men are equally guilty? Come Dora, this is Nigeria of the seventies, not of the fifties. We must understand, and we must learn fast.'

'If Chris had been faithful, if he had not been cruel. If he had treated me well in Hamburg, I would not have had anything to do with Tunde.'

'I could say that of Ernest too. I think we were over-sheltered by the good missionaries. They were good in their own ways, but they did not prepare us for the kind of life we would be called upon to live in Nigeria of the seventies,' said Rose.

'No, we should leave the white missionaries out of it. Our own mothers did not prepare us for it either,' said Dora.

'When I was talking with a group of women the other day, one of them, who was a doctorate degree in history and is unmarried, agreed with us that the society was sick. She said very heatedly, "If husbands run around with other men's wives, why should not their wives do the same?" ' Rose paused and went on again:

'You see, Dora, we in Nigeria are in a kind of cultural melting pot. We have moved too fast since independence. Think of the colonial era. Things did not move too fast but we were sure where we were going. Since independence, we have had a civilian regime, a military regime, and civil war all between 1960 to 1974.

'Think of our culture again at this period. Even before the British came to rule us, there were so many primitive societies in our country, untouched by any outside influence. In one primitive society, if a man caught his wife with another man, he cut off the man's head, a very glorious action indeed! In another primitive society, if a man caught another man with his lover, he cut off the head of the man who tampered with his lover. In yet another primitive society, a husband could give his wife in order to find favour from another man.

'So what has changed? Our values. A man knows now that if he catches his wife in a most compromising situation, the law forbids him to cut off the head of the intruder. So he is restrained.'

'It is a difficult situation, I know,' said Dora. 'I am sad because my marriage failed. And I must be frank with you, Rose, if Chris comes back today and shows penitence, I'll go back to him.

'You will, knowing you as I do. If we say we are Christians, we must practise Christianity, that is, we must forgive those who have wronged us. Enough of all this, Dora. Now tell me about Tunde, what kind of person is he?'

'Rose, I came to ask your opinion. Tunde has asked me to marry him, but I have told him to give me time to think things over. Rose, I am a bit frightened about Tunde's ways. As I grow to like him, I find it more difficult to live with him. Tunde is a difficult person to live with. He lives alone in a big house. He has no domestic servants, he has no visitors, he discourages his colleagues from visiting him. When they pay him a visit, he does not return the visit. He has set ways of doing things. He won't discuss his family. His wife was killed in a motor accident along with his youngest child some five years ago, and since then he has not recovered from the shock. He blames himself because he drove the car on that fateful day.

'You see he had quarrelled with his wife on that day and he was in a temper, his wife had told him not to drive, but he refused. He drove and he killed her and his child. The guilt weighs heavily on him night and day. It seems nothing can wipe away that guilt. It is said that his wife was a very good woman. They were very much in love. Nobody has been able to convince Tunde that he does not have to torture himself in that way; that he was not at fault.

'Well, Rose, you see my predicament! Such a man with that kind of guilt hanging over him will be very difficult to live with. And I have to submerge my personality to be able to cope, because I believe that in Nigeria today if a woman marries a difficult husband, and if she wants the marriage to last, she has to be prepared to take a lot. She has to be prepared to receive insults from all and sundry. She has to ignore all her husband's shortcomings. She has to give and give and continue to give. For you see, our men are very touchy these days. They lord it over their wives, and they laugh at the ideal husband who listens and respects his wife.

'So I am in a dilemma. I want a husband and not a lover. Here is Tunde, and I know in my heart that I cannot stand him as a husband. If I agree to marry him, he will start clamping down on me and will not give me any breathing space. He will start controlling my business, and become authoritative.

'Before I came to you, I gave Tunde a deep thought. I meditated, I prayed, but I have not reached any worthwhile conclusion. A lot about him worries me. His eating habits, his orderliness which almost amounts to a ritual. Sometimes, when I am with him, I see an invisible set of rules which he hands to whoever tries to come close, even me, saying in

102

effect, "These are my rules, take them or get out."

'He washes his clothes, irons them, buys his food in the supermarket once a month. He labels everything neatly and piles them neatly into the freezer. He cannot eat any oil that is not imported. I used palm oil to cook for him once and he politely refused to eat, and since then, I have not had the courage to cook for him. He has a way of cooking his vegetables, a way of eating his fruits, and no other way will do.

'His day begins at five in the morning. He says his prayers, does his exercises while one of his numerous classical pieces is playing. And you know Rose, no matter how much I pretend, I will never appreciate those classical records. After his exercises, he goes downstairs, makes himself a cup of coffee, using a percolator. Once he allowed me to make him coffee, I did, when I brought it upstairs, he smiled, gave me a peck on the cheek, took me downstairs and proceeded to lecture me on how to brew coffee. When I did not get it right at the third attempt, I gave up.

'The coffee made, he comes upstairs, adds three lumps of sugar, no milk, and proceeds to drink it with great relish, listening to his records. At first I tried to drink his coffee; you know I don't drink coffee; he told me politely that the percolator makes just two cups and if I wanted coffee, I should make my own.

'This ritual ends at six in the morning. Then he turns off the player, and switches on to BBC. After the news, he goes back to bed. All this time not a word, not even good morning. Then at seven he goes to the bathroom, spends ten minutes there, dresses up and by seven thirty he comes to the room to collect his car-key. It is then that he realises that someone is in the house. He says one or two things, mostly irrelevant, tells you when he will return. Then he makes one hilarious remark that sends you almost rolling on the ground with laughter.'

Rose paid attention as Dora narrated her life with Tunde. 'He leaves the office at four o'clock and when he returns

103

home depending on the traffic situation, he parks the car neatly in the garage, then he comes upstairs. There he kisses me and we go down and have the first meal of the day. He eats very little, then he drinks his beer, and reads his newspapers, while I stay in the background not knowing what do with myself.

'He never leaves the house again unless it is absolutely necessary. He reads his numerous books or listens to more records. When he is in a good mood he tells you his experiences at the office – otherwise I doze off at nine o'clock then at about one in the morning, he wakes me up for sex. I protest, but he is sorry, that is the only time he can make love. What a man!

'Then just out of the blue, he asked me once if I would marry him. The proposal gave me a jolt. Marriage? To Tunde? I am most inadequate. And besides, I have not divorced my husband in the law courts. But more importantly, Tunde is not my type of man. He is more your type, the bookish one. I am a trader more or less. Tunde wants someone like you, orderly existence, university graduate and all that. So you see . . .' She was quiet again. She had said enough.

Rose was fascinated! 'Tunde sounds romantic to me. If I were in your shoes, I would marry him without hesitation. My, Dora that's the kind of man I want for myself. Surely you don't want the noisy type who goes out every night and returns home drunk, and beats you up because you did not wait for him to return so you can give him his meal? You don't want the kind of man who will return home with "friends" who eat up all your food, drink all your beer and your well boiled and filtered water in the fridge?. . .

'Before I go on, you have not told me about Tunde's relatives.'

'He has not mentioned any, and I have not asked.'

'Ask him, not that it matters. One who behaves in that way will make sure his relatives are far, far away.

'Dora, I am your friend, your childhood friend. I am not

104

married, you have married. I don't know what advice to give. My instinct tells me you should marry him. My instinct tells me that if I see anybody who can give me a child, I shall damn all consequences, and go ahead whether he is married or not. But Tunde is not married. And technically you are not, so what is your problem? You should be flattered that he is proposing. But you have not mentioned anything about Tunde's financial situation. How well off is he?'

'Honestly, I don't know,' said Dora.

'You should find out. What does he do for a living?' asked Rose.

'Well, he works in Port Harcourt with a construction company. He is in Aba now because his company is constructing the Umuahia-Port Harcourt Highway.'

'That's a good job. Find out his attitude towards money. Does he give generously? Who wants a man who is stingy? I hate men who shirk their financial obligations.'

'But Rose you know me too well. I have always worked and earned my money. I don't mind whether I am given or not but . . . You are right, I should find out.'

'Remember, I am still single. I believe that if you say you are the bread-winner, and in that token lord it over me, you jolly well have to provide for your home. However, that is neither here nor there. I know you have not changed since school days. I know that once you are in love with a man, other things are secondary. I don't think you are really in love with Tunde. If you were, you would go all out. I know you'.

'You have hit the nail on the head. You see, I am not sure what I feel for him. I divorced Chris by native law and custom out of anger and frustration. If I were sure of Tunde I would not have come to you,' said Dora truthfully.

'You are right. I envy you, and I love you. Right now, I have nobody. When I spent that short time with Olu in London, the greatest pleasure I had was waking up in the mornings and seeing Olu by my side. It was short-lived, but I would do anything in my power to re-live that experience all

105

over again. We talked, we listened to the news, we listened to music, he ordered breakfast. We sat facing each other eating breakfast. These are little things which married women take for granted, but which we single women value.

'Look at the account of Tunde's day which you have given me. You talk of your hilarious laughter nearly every morning before he goes to work. Do you know that there are too many people today who cannot laugh or make others laugh. Tunde makes you laugh, I envy you Dora. Many people have forgotten how to laugh, because few people can make them laugh. The white man in his wisdom goes to great lengths to make films which make people laugh. Laughter they say is a great medicine.'

'Rose you are right. But I get all my amusement from the customers who buy from me.'

'True, but it is not the same. You need someone like Tunde who will help you with your business. You need a man. Your Managers will not do. They are not close to you,' said Rose.

'You are right, but perhaps, who knows Chris may come back.'

The two friends were silent for a while, each in deep thought. Rose thought they should terminate this discussion. Dora thought the same and broke the silence, 'You have not told me about Ernest.'

'What is there to tell? I have not heard from him ever since he made that proposal. I understand that he played a major role in London during the war, organising speeches and meetings for the Biafrans who had come on peace talks. It was said that he visited Biafra twice during the war, and that when the war ended, he went to Zambia where he worked. All this information I gathered from his friends and his mother. But what baffled me was that he did not write or visit me.

'One day, Comfort visited me and told me that she saw Ernest in a restaurant in Lagos, with a very pretty woman whom he introduced as his wife.'

'No,' said Dora.

'Yes, so Comfort told me. Ernest told her that he was on a business trip. She asked him whether he had seen me. He pretended as if he did not know whom Comfort was talking about. But you know Comfort, she said, come on, Rose of course, ACMGS and Grammar School. Oh, Ernest exclaimed and said he did not know that I was in Lagos.'

'When was this?' asked Dora.

'It must be in 1972 or early 1973, I cannot quite remember. Then one day my Secretary told me that Ernest called when I was not in the office. He did not leave a telephone number or an address. About a month after his visit to my office, Ernest's mother came to Lagos and asked me whether I had seen him. I hadn't seen him. Then she began to cry. Why was she crying? She would not tell me. All she kept saying was that she was disappointed in Ernest, that her son Ernest had let her down. You know me, since she did not want to talk, I did not want to force her to talk. She left after staying with me for four days. That was the last I heard about Ernest. No letter, no telephone calls, nothing.'

'There must be something in Europe that makes our men behave in that strange way,' said Dora.

'Whatever it is, why should Ernest come to me after his problem with the Irish girl, propose marriage and disappear into thin air?'

'Maybe the war spoilt his plans.'

'But the war ended in 1970, Dora, and we are now in 1974.'

'I know. Have an open mind about it,' said Dora.

'Of course, what else can I do. Now to Chinwe:

'I received Chinwe's letter just before I travelled to the States on vacation. Dora you must go to the States' she said.

'Of course I must go,' said Dora, 'but you see, in the private sector you hardly have time for anything other than your business. You trust no one to handle it when you are away. I love to travel as you know, but . . .'

'I understand. I went on an excursion tour organised by a group in the United Kingdom who call themselves "The Group for Peace in the World". I don't know who gave my name to this group, but I was invited to join them on a vacation in Los Angeles.

'You are not listening,' said Rose.

'I am all ears,' said Dora. 'Go on, but get something from the fridge, I want to eat. Anything to chew, and a glass of water.'

It was like old times again. They used to drink gari and water after lights out, and enjoyed it. 'Tell me why don't I enjoy gari, water and coconuts these days?' asked Rose.

'We were growing children in those days, anything edible was delicious, and remember we were always hungry.' Rose brought some fish and water, and went on: 'This group is made up of quite some characters mainly aged men and women who are very active in their adult lives. Growing old, they begin to look at the world with a kind of nostalgia. The good old days were no more. The world economic recession stared them in the face, and they became almost strangers in their own societies where they were born and bred. So the bright ones among them got the Group organised worldwide, got cheaper fares and accommodation for their conferences and their preoccupation was peace in the world, averting the global third world war that would destroy mankind.

'I wondered whose bright idea it was to invite me to be a member. I abhor war or any other confrontation all right, but I have never made my opinions known to the public, not being the soap-box type. However it was not a bad vacation. I met a rather extraordinary American lady from Texas who invited me to her home in Houston. She claimed to be an educationist and that her method of teaching the art of reading and writing was the best in the whole world, but that she was keeping it a secret until the United States government talks business with her. She had travelled round the world twelve times and had met practically all the heads of states of the countries she visited.

'At her age, and I would put it at eighty, she was still active, still working on her reading and writing methods. She said she was not a millionaire but that she lived like one, because all her relatives were millionaires making money in oil and big business.

'She drove me all over Houston and I had a lovely time, but the people I saw were old people like her and I was introduced to all of them as the "Princess from Africa". I told her I was not a princess but she said I looked like one and therefore I must be one.

'When she was not with me, I took a taxi and went to the shops. I discovered that there was a large Nigerian population in Houston. The taxi driver who took me back to my flat was a Nigerian. When I saw him, he was the first in the queue. He spoke with an American accent, but I looked at him, and asked him in Ibo, "Are you from Nigeria?" He replied in Ibo, "I am an Ibo from Nkwere". There and then he gave me the names of some students I was likely to know while in Houston. He was a student but had to pay his way through. The only job they could get in Houston was taxi-driving. The girls were luckier, they could be employed in offices, but not the boys. Life was rough, they knew it, and yet they sent money back home urging their brothers to come and rough it with them.

'One of the Nigerians whose sister I knew invited me to his home. It was a modest home, and he had his young wife who had been "posted" to him from home, and their six month old baby. He told me he did it because it was dangerous for him to marry an American black or white. Nigerians, he said did not treat their American wives well. These American girls bent over backwards to love them and to help them financially. They used these girls, and abandoned them as soon as they had their immigrant visas.

'There was a case in which a Nigerian student was shot dead by his wife in a night club because she suspected that he was about to abandon her. Nothing came out of it. She had "witnesses" who testified that she shot him in self defence. She was the next of kin and was therefore responsible for his burial arrangements. She said that while her husband was alive, he told her that if he died in Houston, he should be

109

cremated. Now who talks of cremation in Nigeria and Ibo land of all places? In Nigeria we don't burn our dead, we bury them amidst the booming of guns, the beating of drums, great show of grief. And there was this poor fellow burnt, ashes scattered to the winds, all in the name of being educated in the United States of America.'

'Say that again,' said Dora. 'I want to hear that again. I pray Chris does not end up like that. I know he is being kept by the German woman, the hot-headed children of Hitler, that's what I call them. I am afraid of them. And Chris is there. In Hamburg of all places. Doing what? Studying German language at old age. What will he do with the language at his age?'

'Don't worry Dora, all will be well. I was telling you of my vacation. It gave me peace and tranquillity, I rested and I relaxed. I just felt the pressure going away, as if someone was washing them away with a kind of supernatural power. I did not know how tired I was until I arrived in Houston. Sometimes I slept for more than twelve hours at at time. If only we Nigerians realise what it is to have a vacation, the death rate will be minimal. The other day, a company driver told me that he did not know what it was like to rest, that he did not need rest. He could drive all day, just stopping eating and drinking and going on again. When I told him that in civilised countries that bus drivers drove for only six hours at a time, he told me that they were lazy. Is there any wonder that the accident rate is high in Nigeria?'

They finally slept, and in the morning while Rose prepared for work, Dora talked to her about so many things. She wanted to see Agnes. Rose told her that it was easy because she had her telephone number and that she would call her in the office. Dora stayed at home while Rose went to work. She did the cooking, rested and waited for her friend to return. She was going to talk to her about her daughter Chinwe who was getting out of hand. That her marriage did not succeed did not mean that Chinwe's marriage should not succeed. She wanted Chinwe to stay put in her husband's home whatever happened. Dora had been so worried about Chinwe that she had sent her off to pay Rose a visit in Lagos. She was to talk over the marital problems with her and seek advice. When Chinwe, who was fond of Rose, paid her auntie a visit, she bared her heart to her. Rose listened attentively, but was at a loss for what to tell her. She was almost referred to now as a spinster, dangerously approaching forty two years. What advice would she give a young girl of about twenty two with children, who had the misfortune of marrying an irresponsible man. As far as Rose was concerned, she was just in the position that priests find themselves in when they are faced with this kind of problem. All she did was preach to Chinwe. She told her of the advantages she would derive from merely staying with her husband and carrying on her trade.

But Chinwe was not consoled. Her husband had already brought in a seventeen year old girl to her matrimonial home and she had moved out. Rose told her it was wrong for her to have moved out. But she said she would rather die than have a seventeen year old girl share her home with her. She was young she said, and would find her happiness elsewhere. She could start all over again at her age, but her own mother could not because of her age. She would work hard like her mother and she would make it to the top. And when Rose asked about her children, she said they would understand when they grew up. And besides, she was too young to sacrifice her life and happiness for her children when she was still young.

Rose came back and the friends continued talking. 'Agnes was not in the office but I left a note for her, I am sure she will call me at home. Yes,' she went on. 'Chinwe is mature and I was happy talking to her. Whatever we do, we must not impose our will on our children. Of course she is young, but then we are in the seventies, not the fifties. We have to make allowances for all that happened when we were young children and now.

'I was angry at Ernest on account of the Irish girl. I did not

111

think of him in his predicament. I thought only of myself. He needed support at the time. He needed understanding and love. I did not give him any of those. I revelled in my hurt and I refused to forgive him, and now here I am, close to forty three, no child, no Ernest, no husband and no lover. You are worried about what people will say. Nonsense. Give Chinwe a chance. Let her live her own life, you have lived and are still living yours.'

'I understand you, Rose, I do. But tell me, why did Chinwe's husband come to me to tell me about the girl?'

'Oh, did he come to see you?'

'Yes he did. I was glad that he did. I knew he found it difficult to come to me but he did. I knew he came out of guilt. That was why I begged Chinwe to forgive him. Our men don't normally behave in that way especially when they have a bit of money which they never expected would come their way. He told me he still cared for Chinwe, but that he could not help himself. He had taken all the titles that he could take as a successful man. It was not right, for him to have just one wife. So he asked me to see with him and welcome the brand new wife.'

'Yes, I remember Chinwe mentioned something about what you are saying, and . . .' The telephone rang and Rose went to answer it. 'It must be Agnes,' she said as she picked it up. 'Agnes, good. You received my message. Yes, Dora is here. She wants to see you. Oh is that right, Comfort is in town. I thought she went to Accra. I see, she was in London. When can you come? All right, we will be expecting you. Dora does not want to speak to you over the telephone. She wants to see you. So we shall be expecting you tomorrow. Bye.' Rose went to the bedroom. 'Do you want something to drink?' Dora wanted beer and she brought it and they went on talking.

'Yes as I was saying, Chinwe told me about this girl. She came to her home posing as her husband's first cousin. In her naivety, she asked no questions. She treated her like she treated the relations of her husband, with love and respect.

112

She went out of her way to buy her presents and to take her out to see her friends. Little did she know that her husband was having an affair with his "cousin" under her own roof. When she discovered that the girl was expecting a baby, she told her husband, and he said nothing. She gave no thought to it again until a friend of hers told her without mincing words that her husband was responsible for the girl's pregnancy. It hurt her badly. She had been a good wife. She was only twenty three. What did her husband want? If he wanted more children, she was prepared to give him ten in less than ten years.'

'Chinwe told me,' Dora said nodding.

'She did?' asked Rose.

'She did. I know it hurt her. It is not so much the adultery as the deceit that is hurting Chinwe, I know, but still, I don't want her to leave her husband, because of the effect it will have on her younger sister who is not yet married. Soon people will say that my daughters are incapable of marriage, that they are following my footsteps.'

'Even when they know that it is neither your fault nor Chinwe's fault.'

'You talk as if you never went home. Lagos has sort of detribalised you, that you no longer think like people at home.'

'I understand you. Mark you, I am not holding any brief for Chinwe. I am not asking her to leave her husband. All I am saying is that I understand her problem and that you should try and understand it as well. Let her think out her salvation her own way. Don't interfere. Allow her to make her own mistakes. She will be more capable to cope with her own mistakes than the ones you make for her. That's all I am saying.'

The two women knew that marriage in Nigeria in the seventies was quite different from marriage of the forties. The women thought that their men were chickens who were manipulated by their mothers, sisters and all the clan. Rose told of a man she knew very well and complained that his wife ill-treated him because he had neither a mother nor a sister to give her a good fight. The man did not know the implication of what he was saying. He single handedly could not control his wife, could not look her in the face and say 'Woman, enough is enough'. He needed female relations in the family to do that for him.

Chapter 8

Shortly after Dora's visit, Rose learnt that Chinwe had left her husband and was engaged in beer-parlour business. This was hardly an ideal business for a young woman who had left her husband. Dora, who was a lazy letter writer wrote a lengthy letter to her friend Rose and lamented her daughter's waywardness. Rose was not happy about this. Any young girl who carried on that kind of business, was of course a prostitute. That was it. The business was a cover up for prostitution, and not even an angel would make it respectable.

Rose wrote back to her friend to console her. 'Who are we really to judge and condemn? Are we righteous ourselves? Have we not done those things which we should not have done and failed to do the ones we should have done? All we should do is pray to God for his mercy and forgiveness.'

Before her letter reached Dora, Comfort paid her a visit. She told her that Chinwe had married a married man. She endorsed it. She gave her blessings to it. Comfort said that she would encourage her daughters to go where the money and the security was. As far as she was concerned, the society was rotten and she was not going to be an angel among devils. 'This man will look after Chinwe,' Comfort said. But Rose was doubtful. 'If Chinwe could marry a married man, why did she leave her husband? You see Comfort, I don't understand. I would rather have Chinwe stick to her first husband. Why this mess now? Why this complication? I don't understand it.'

'I do,' said Comfort. 'The man is wealthy. He throws his money about. He has already built a house for Chinwe'.

'A house? When did she meet him?'

'I am not quite sure, but I think they met not quite nine months ago.'

'Nine months? The business must be lucrative. A rich man meets a young mother at a beer-parlour, who recently left her husband and after nine months builds her a house. That is quite tempting I must say. So what you are saying Comfort is that Chinwe married this man because of his wealth.'

'Exactly, Rose, don't be daft. Your missionary way of thinking has not left you yet. I tell you, I shall encourage my own daughters to do the same. The men in question could be old enough to be their own fathers, for all I care.'

'You mean that?' asked Rose.

'Of course I do. The men – filthy men I call them – have nothing to do with their money. If they are so foolish as to spend it in that way, why should I stop them?' said Comfort.

'Tell me, who is giving more in this relationship, the girls or the men?'

'The girls, of course.'

'You are damn right. Comfort, I like your honesty. You are free of hypocrisy. The girls give their bodies, their youth, their vitality to the filthy sugar daddies. Where I disagree with you is when you say that you will encourage your daughters to do the same.'

'Rose, you have been a romantic girl since school days. You have had everything. I mean, you have never lacked anything. If you came from a family that is so poor that they cannot afford three square meals day, then you will understand what I mean. I happen to be from that kind of family. You did not know it while we were at school. I was clever, I hid my poverty very well. While in school, when I saw people like you and Cecilia and Bridget, I vowed to myself that if it meant stealing, I will steal so my children would not be poor.'

'I now understand,' said Rose. 'If you were better born like myself for instance, you would behave differently, I mean you won't encourage your daughters to . . .'

116

'I am not too sure about that though, I must tell you, but . . .'

'I see,' said Rose.

'What I am trying to put across to you is that I can understand Dora's daughter more than you or Dora do. Chinwe has learnt a lot from her mother's problems. What she is doing is reacting to them. Her mother was so good to her father, but see how shabbily her mother was treated. What Chinwe is trying to say is this, "Mother I cannot take what you have taken from father. I am going to have my own back. No man is going to hold me to ransom, and . . ."'

'In short, what she is doing is an act of revenge?' asked Rose.

'Not exactly, I should say defiance, that's the appropriate word. She will get over it soon. If I have the time, I shall visit Dora and talk to her. Chinwe is playing a game. But she must be careful. I think I should talk to her as well. This is the time for her to grab what she can get from this man, and get out'.

'And get out?' asked Rose.

Comfort laughed a mirthless laugh. 'Yes, and get out. No relationship, especially this kind, lasts forever. So Chinwe should make haste and get out. My guess is that she will go back to her husband, when she discovers that all that glitters is not gold, when the novelty of her new found love wears off. I know she loves her husband. She entered that marriage with the enthusiasm of an adolescent genuinely in love with her husband. And when she had that raw deal, like the child she was, she left. If she were older, she would have stayed.'

Comfort was right. Chinwe was 'married' for only eighteen months. Her husband was not as wealthy as Chinwe believed. He was a contractor, and when he won a contract from the army, he was given mobilisation fees which he squandered, without even making the foundation of the building. When the regime of Murtala Mohammed came to power, his power base was no more. So he had contracts for supplying sand and gravel. Chinwe did get out at the right time. She lied to friends that she got out because her husband

117

neglected his own children while she was married to him. She was deeply touched, she said. A man who could neglect his own children was not worth taking seriously, therefore she left.

Like her mother, she was industrious. She closed the beer-parlour and got herself a contract worth one million naira from the new military rulers. She worked hard and was able to finish the job in record time and was paid. But Dora was not happy. She had made it by dint of hard work no doubt, but she wanted a good home for her daughter. Dora was not interested in material success. She was not impressed that her daughter could handle a one million naira job. She as well as Rose did not approve of a society where it is possible for young women of twenty four or twenty five to boast of possessing a Mercedes Benz, big business associates overseas, expense account paid, credit cards and so on, without a husband. At forty what would this brand of women be? What was left to be achieved?

But Chinwe's husband surprised her when he began to visit her, two years after she left him. One evening he visited her, and stayed so long that it was too late to leave. She made him a bed in the guest room, and left him to sleep alone. Another time her husband came and saw one of her men friends and made a disgraceful scene. She quietly took her car key and disappeared. When she returned, her husband was still in the house. 'You must know that you are my wife. So stop behaving as if you are a free woman. I have not divorced you, neither have you divorced me. So you must behave. You are a mother, what will your children think of you behaving in this way?'

The next day, Chinwe went to a laywer. She wanted divorce, and she wanted the custody of her children. She wanted no maintenance money for her children.

'But you need the money,' said the lawyer.

'No, I don't need his money. I want my children and my peace of mind and freedom.' She won her case and was free.

Chinwe had done the right thing. Her generation was

doing better than her mother's own. Her generation was telling the men, that there are different ways of living one's life fully and fruitfully. They are saying that women have options. Their lives cannot be ruined because of a bad marriage. They have a choice, a choice to set up a business of their own, a choice to marry and have children, a choice to marry or divorce their husbands. Marriage is not THE only way.

'Oh Tinu, what a day! Has anyone called from London or New York?'

'No Madam,' Tinu replied.

'Isn't it hot? What a day. Isn't the airconditioner working again?'

'No madam. The workmen were called, but they have not come.'

'Whose idea was it about giving out the maintenance of the air-conditioners to a contractor? It was not my idea. Whose bright idea was it Tinu, do you know?'

'No madam. It was decided at the meeting of the executives,' said Tinu.

'When are we having another meeting of the executives? I must tell them that the contractor has not performed at all. Can you get a table fan. My, it is hot.

'I cannot understand Nigerian architects. Why? We are in the tropics. We have two seasons, the rainy season and the dry season. It is hot throughout the year, whether dry or wet. And yet our architects design buildings as if air conditioners grew on trees, as if they have never heard of what is called cross ventilation, the walls are so thick, one would think that Nigeria is the earthquake region. You cannot work in your office because the air-conditioner has broken down. I hate fans. Fans give me headache and cold.

'Okay, put it over there,' Rose said to Tinu. 'Yes, over there, far away so that I can finish with these papers and go to the airport.'

119

'Are you still going to the airport?' asked Tinu.

'Yes of course, why?'

'No, I was just wondering.'

'Stop wondering, I am going.' She looked up at her secretary. She wore a sad face.

'Why, Tinu what is wrong? Are you well? Your children?'

For an answer Tinu gave her a copy of the *Daily Times*. She took it from her, and her heart missed several beats. She looked at her. 'Page twelve,' she said to her boss.

Rose opened page twelve, and there it was. She saw Ernest and a young woman on page twelve. She also saw a London policeman on that page. Then she read the caption. The man whose name was Mr. John Davis from Liberia was none other than Ernest. The young woman with him was Zizi, Agnes' daughter. She was of no fixed address. They were both caught at Heathrow Airport with four suitcases containing Indian hemp and dangerous drugs.

Rose looked up and saw Tinu, goose pimples were all over her arms, there were tears in her eyes. 'Wipe away your tears Tinu. What will be will be.'

'I am sorry madam.'

'Thank you. Wipe away your tears. Interesting I have none to shed.'

'Can I take you home?'

'No thank you, but cancel all my engagements for today.'

When Tinu shut the door she came face to face with Agnes. 'Good morning. Please, I would like to see your boss, Rose. I am Mrs. Egemba. I am sure she would like to see me.'

'Do you have an appointment?'

'No. Please just mention my name. I am sure she would like to see me. Here show her this. I have come to talk to her about this,' she thrust the *Daily Times* into Tinu's hand.

Tinu picked up the telephone, and spoke into it. She replaced it and asked the lady to follow her. She was surprised to see how composed Rose was. She made coffee and left them.

The two women faced each other. Neither was in any

mood for small talk. 'You have seen today's *Daily Times*?'
Agnes asked.

'Yes, of course I have.'

'The girl with Ernest is my daughter.'

'No!'

'That's why I have come. Rose it was all my fault. If I had put my foot down, I would have stopped my daughter from going astray. I am to blame, and now I am paying for my failure. Elizabeth is my only child who has refused to be straight. She was a child who did not give me any trouble until she was six years old. Her promiscuity was so much that I worried that there was something psychologically wrong with her. She refused to sleep with my other children in their room. She disliked the company of young people like herself. I noticed it all and gently talked to her, but she paid no heed.

'She has good qualities. She can, without help, wash, iron, clean everything in the house. Her cooking was better than mine and her other sister. She did these domestic chores so effortlessly that I consoled myself by saying that she could do some home economics in one of the centres in Lagos. But before Elizabeth was fifteen, she left home and lived with a woman known to be the proprietress of a brothel. When I went there to bring her back, she told me that I was no better than the proprietress of the brothel. I was hurt. She did not stop there. She told me to straighten my ways first before bothering about her. She wanted to know my explanation for abandoning her father, while I prostituted in Lagos. It was after that incident that I brought her father to my flat in Ikoyi. It was in this brothel that she got the crazy name – Zizi.

'When Elizabeth was eighteen, I was knocked up by a police man in the early hours of the morning. A criminal whom the police knew was an armed robber was seen with my daughter just before a robbery. I pleaded with the policeman, but he refused to let her go until I offered him one thousand naira bribe. But he would not accept a cheque. I gave him my gold bracelet and asked him to come to my office the next day for the money.

'My daughter was of good behaviour for two months. I could see her good qualities manifesting themselves again and I was pleased. But one day when I returned from work, she had gone. She left a note saying she was a businesswoman and time meant a good deal to her. Before I could live that one down, she visited me in Mercedez Benz. She had bought it and she had brought champagne to toast the car. "Have you anything to do with armed robbers?" I asked in desperation. She laughed at me and drove away. Not long after, she brought a man she called her husband. I took her into my room and questioned her. She gave nothing away. Oh she liked the man. He had other wives of course. But they don't bother her. She lives in her own flat. She was not a child any more and was capable of taking care of herself.

'I prayed hard to God. I asked him to forgive me all my sins, and help me help my daughter. I saw the "prophets" in Lagos and prayed to them to assist me in praying that God should help my prodigal daughter. I fasted, I sacrificed, but my wayward daughter remained wayward.

'Then one day my daughter came to my office with a man she introduced to me as her boy-friend who was from Zambia. I thought he was a Zambian. But I later discovered that he was not only a Nigerian but Ernest. I did not want to let Ernest know that I knew him while we were in school. I did not want to embarrass him in any way. My daughter told me she was travelling to London with Ernest the next morning. She wanted to be a secretary, work for Ernest for a while, and then set up her own business.

'Oh my God, where did I go wrong? God why did you give me this daughter? I said nothing to her. She left with Ernest. I wondered why she came to see me in the first place. Did she just want to inform me or did she have an ulterior motive? One never knows with the new generation of girls. My! Rose, we were different during our own time. If I think too much of Elizabeth, I will be a mental case. No, she must not upset me. She must not. After all I have three other children. I have my

122

life to live. I have a duty towards my other children and my husband as well. I was a victim of child marriage, but I made the best of a bad job. Good luck to Elizabeth. But can one really turn one's back on one's daughter? Can one disown one's daughter? Can I write in the papers – Mrs . . . so and so is no longer the mother of Miss so and so? I can't do that. She is my daughter and will never be anybody's daughter but mine.

'Rose, I should have come earlier than now. I should have told you about Ernest and my daughter. Comfort told me quite a lot about Ernest. She said you were crazy to give Ernest a thought at all. Didn't you know what type of business Ernest did? I did not ask her the nature of Ernest's business because I was not emotionally prepared to know. Again I was not sure that she knew that Ernest knew my daughter.' She paused.

'Go on,' encouraged Rose.

'Since the war ended, Ernest has been involved in trafficking in hemp and dangerous drugs.'

'Go on.'

Agnes was not receiving the response that she expected. She thought she had misfired. She should not have said what she had just said. 'Rose,' she began, 'we can organise their defence. We can help them.'

'You and me?' asked Rose.

'Yes, you and me.'

'Zizi is your daughter. What is Ernest to me? Agnes what has come over you. I thought we were friends. I was never married to Ernest.'

'But you are taking care of his mother,' Agnes said weakly.

'Yes I am, on compassionate grounds, understand me? Please kindly leave my office, I beg you.'

She got up and went to the door, indicating that the interview was over.

But even then in spite of what she told Agnes, Rose did an extraordinary thing. She went to Ernest's home and brought

123

his mother to Lagos for fear that local people would hear and make life miserable for her. She did not know what motivated her action. Was it pity for Ernest's mother or what? It was a stupid thing to do, but having done it, she could do nothing about it. Then she sat down and wrote to Dora:

'My Dear Dora,

Dora, is there anyone who has the kind of problem that I have? Do you not think that it is high time I went to a palmist? Or perhaps I should go to Ijebu to be told what to do so that my good fortune will begin to manifest itself again. Tinu often tells me to go to Ijebu. Her own sister had so much misfortune like the ones I am having, so a friend recommended Ijebu to her; she went, and now everything has changed for her. She earned a promotion in her job. She got married and she now has a child. My Nanny has told me so too, and I am thinking seriously of taking their advice. But Dora one has to believe, one has to have faith before one can have positive results. My upbringing does not value that kind of approach.'

Then she told Dora about Ernest, his mother and Agnes' visit. She was now landed with Ernest's mother and she wondered why she did such a rash thing by asking her to come to Lagos.

Shortly after this letter was posted to Dora, she got a letter from Dora telling her that she had heard from Chris, and that he was expected back in Nigeria next year.

Chapter 9

Agnes regretted her visit to Rose. She telephoned her as soon as she got back to her office and apologised – Rose accepted her apology. Then she set to work. She swore that she would defend her daughter even if it meant selling all she had. Her daughter would not languish in a London jail. She found out the source of the publication in the newspaper. She paid money, and so killed further information on the subject in the newspaper.

Then she made inquiries using the people she knew in business, and as luck would have it, she was given a name and an address in Lagos. The person who bore the name happened to be the man Elizabeth brought home as her husband. Agnes launched an offensive immediately. 'You cannot be hiding away here when my daughter is languishing in jail. I will expose you, I will go to a newspaper office as soon as I leave here if you will not do anything for my daughter. Now.'

The man was frightened. Things hadn't moved according to plan. He wanted to lie low for a little while before he started his business again. He did not know the source of the betrayal in Heathrow and he was so low in spirit. Again he had not heard from the leader of his syndicate who was based in London. He pleaded with Agnes to have patience. The syndicate will never abandon Elizabeth. He liked Elizabeth and no harm will come to her. Agnes must be patient and must keep her mouth shut, and he swore that Elizabeth will not be in jail for long. Agnes should wait for him to come to her as soon as he possibly could.

After two weeks the man visited Agnes, and gave her a passport and a return ticket to London, a parcel and a London telephone number. He told her to phone the number as soon as she arrived at Heathrow, and he got up. Agnes asked him to sit down. 'Look mister, what do you call yourself?'

'Mr. Johnson,' he said, surprised.

'Mr. Johnson, sit down and listen to me. I don't belong to your syndicate, so don't mistake me for my daughter. I demand to be treated respectfully.' Mr. Johnson wanted to protest but Agnes stopped him and went on. 'You cannot hand me a forged passport and a parcel and a telephone number and say, no questions should be asked. What do you take me for? If you used my daughter, do you think that you can use me as well? No mister, you are in the wrong coach. What am I going to London for? Who is sending me to London? What is in the parcel? You take me for an errand woman? You must be joking. You . . . you think I have come to join your syndicate? I want my daughter out of jail. Tell your syndicate, I want my daughter out of jail or else there will be trouble.'

Mr. Johnson worried. It could be seen in his face. So Agnes gained more confidence, and lashed out at him and threatened to call in the police. The threat was a big joke. Police, in this case? Agnes would rather die. But then an idea occurred to her at the time she was lashing out at Mr. Johnson. Why not go again to the source that gave her his address. Perhaps they would help her.

So Agnes faced Mr. Johnson: 'I have my own passport and I can afford to travel to London if I want to. In two weeks I want to hear something positive about my daughter. I want her freed. And from my contact,' she emphasised the last word, though she had no contact, 'I know that your syndicate can free her.'

When he left visibly shaken, Agnes was afraid that he would send killers to murder her, so she contacted a security organisation who watched her house night and day. But this precaution was not enough. She moved to Comfort's house. And God bless Comfort, she took her in without much ado. Then she went back to her first source who asked her to go to London. There she learnt that Ernest and her daughter were not in fact in jail but in protective custody, but that she was not to see them. But she spoke to her daughter on the telephone. She was assured that no harm will come to her daughter, she must be patient.

About three weeks after Agnes' return from London, she was told that her daughter Elizabeth was free again, and that she would return to her soon. Shortly after that, as she was about to go to bed, there was a knock on her door. She peeped through the window and saw Elizabeth. She opened the door, and Elizabeth threw her arms round her mother. Agnes hugged and hugged her. 'Welcome, my daughter,' Agnes said out of breath. Then she saw a tall man behind her whom Elizabeth said was her fiance.

Then Elizabeth dashed to the kitchen and busied herself cooking. Agnes asked the young man to sit down and offered him beer. He sipped his beer quietly, and when the food came, he ate hungrily.

It was late, so Agnes showed the young man the guest room and slept with her daughter. Elizabeth told her mother that Theo, the young man with her, saved her in London, and they would be married soon. Agnes was too tired and excited to talk. She and her daughter would talk in the morning.

In the morning, Elizabeth told her mother that it was true she and Ernest were caught at Heathrow Airport. Yes it was also true that they had the hemp in their suitcases. But, she said 'What about that?' Everybody does it. We were caught, that's our sin.'

Theo, like Elizabeth was a problem child. When he took Elizabeth to his parents, they were impressed by her. She won their hearts. She took over the cooking as soon as they arrived. She waited upon them and took care of them. Theo's mother swore by her and said her son would marry no other girl than Elizabeth. So the wedding was fixed for twenty-sixth of December. Agnes prayed hard that neither Theo nor her daughter changed their mind before the day. She knew the marriage would not last, but if her daughter could have a child or two before the marriage went on the rocks, it was an achievement. She would then have grandchildren from her dear daughter. Elizabeth might even settle down after the marriage, who knows.

The wedding of Theo and Elizabeth actually took place. Agnes was fabulous. She came with her husband who was quite strong and healthy in spite of his age. She was at her best, and she made sure that her husband wore the latest lace in town. Everybody who was anybody in Bendel State attended the wedding in Benin City.

Elizabeth was simply a beautiful bride. Her wedding dress was bought in Paris and it cost a fortune. She had a bridesmaid and two flower girls who looked like identical twins. She smiled radiantly throughout the ceremony. But the bridegroom nearly ruined the day. He was serious and sulky. His mother took no notice of him and showed everybody that she was happy.

Agnes' children were all present, and they lent colour to the already colourful occasion. At the reception, the Police Band, Victor Uwaifor's band and two 'juju' bands from Lagos were playing. Guests danced, food and wine flowed. Champagne, which was banned, flowed like water. Young boys and girls drank champagne from the bottles. The police who came to keep order were drunk, but then, responsible guests had gone.

Agnes gave her daughter a Mercedes Benz 200, a house in Surulere and a cheque for ten thousand naira. Theo received from his parents a Mercedes Benz 450, a Honda Accord and a flat in London.

Young people gossiped and said Elizabeth was expecting a baby. Others said the marriage was a big joke that Elizabeth was not expecting a baby. The more pessimistic ones gave it just three months.

The couple spent a week in Warri and Lagos and then left for London for their honeymoon. They were to be in London for just two weeks and return to Nigeria. But after a month they did not return. Theo was seen in New York with another beauty. Elizabeth was in London.

The story behind the wedding was that Theo being a problem child was a thorn in the flesh of his parents. He had got mixed up with the underworld in London and in New York. His parents were worried and came to the conclusion that if he got married perhaps he would turn a new leaf.

Theo had told them that he would marry on condition that he chose his bride, and that he would be presented with a Mercedes Benz and the flats in London and New York. His father had agreed, but refused to present him with the flat in New York.

Theo then met Zizi in London when she was in protective custody, liked her and proposed to her. She accepted him. Then Theo told her his conditions for the marriage. To begin with, he did not want to marry anyone. He was too young and he wanted to play around. If Elizabeth could leave him alone, not bother him in any way after the marriage, the London flat which his parents would give him, would be her own. Elizabeth agreed, and so the wedding ceremony was performed.

The reason for Theo's sulkiness during the wedding ceremony was because his father had refused to give him the flat in New York. But before he and his bride left for their honeymoon, his mother had succeeded in persuading her husband to present the New York flat to her son.

The couple spent two glorious weeks in London and they were both bored with each other by the end of the week. So Theo took off to New York with another beauty while Zizi stayed in the London flat which she now called her wedding present from her darling parents-in-law.

On Theo's departure, Zizi was free again to move around and to attend fabulous parties in London. It was at one of these parties that she met Olu – yes

Rose's Olu – and became his lover.

Like Dora, Agnes will have to let her daughter be. Perhaps, Agnes thought, that her daughter's waywardness was her punishment for deserting her husband. In that case she, Agnes, will carry her cross with dignity. But then what was Dora's sin that her daughter was unable to marry successfully?

Agnes telephoned her daughter to find out whether what she heard was true. Elizabeth confirmed that it was true. She had a good quality – she never lied to her mother. Agnes wept and so did Zizi. 'Don't worry mother, I shall be all right. It is better I part with Theo now than later'.

Agnes replied in between sobs. 'Good luck to you Elizabeth. And remember, if ever you are in trouble and require my help, please let me know. I am your mother and my door is always wide open for you to return in prosperity or in adversity.' Then she dropped the telephone and wept and wept.

God help Elizabeth and Theo. They are a part of the world that has gone mad. It is not their fault. It is the fault of their age, and the society. They cannot act differently. One feels the anguish of Agnes, Dora, Ernest's mother, Rose and Theo's parents.

Chris finally returned from Germany, and Dora threw a big party for him, to welcome him home. She asked her friends and business associates to come and rejoice with her for her husband whom she thought would never come back had returned. Now her children have a father. Now no one will ridicule them any more.

In private, she asked no questions. Chris behaved as if he had returned from a week-end, and Dora behaved just the same. And she invited Rose to Aba to welcome Chris.

Rose bought her ticket for Port Harcourt and set out for the airport with a week-end suitcase. When the taxi dropped her, she was confronted by touts who asked her where she was going. Other touts wanted to carry her suit case. She shooed them all away and walked quietly to the 'Departure'

130

hall of the Nigerian Airways. Hundreds of people at the Enugu counter were fighting for their boarding passes. Port Harcourt counter was a bit orderly. She stood waiting for her turn. When it finally reached her turn, she was told that there were no more boarding passes. She had to wait for another flight.

She was upset. Hitherto when she travelled, and she travelled quite a lot inside Nigeria, the office got her ticket, took her to the airport and brought her a boarding pass. She did not know that getting a boarding pass was quite a hassle in Nigeria. 'When is the next flight?' she asked the man at the counter.

'Three o'clock,' he said. 'And we start checking in by two.' Rose looked at her watch. She had to wait for three hours. She stood, thinking of what next to do. Perhaps she should try a private airline at the old airport. Then a tout came and told her that if she paid him twenty naira he would get her a boarding pass. She had made a mistake. She should have travelled to Aba in her car. All she needed was ask the Transport Office to give her a driver.

'I want to see if there is a plane at the old airport,' she said to the tout.

'There is none, Madam. You can try. The taxi driver will take five naira from you and another five naira to bring you back making ten. If you pay me twenty naira I can get you a boarding pass now,' said the tout.

'But they have just said there are no more boarding passes.'

'There will be if I give them ten naira,' the tout said.

'No thank you,' said Rose. She queued again, and eventually got her boarding pass. She waited for the flight at the lounge. There was one hour delay, then two hours delay. Then nothing was heard for another hour. At about nine o'clock there was an announcement. 'Your attention, please. Nigerian airways regrets to announce the cancellation of Flight No. WT 123 to Port Harcourt due to operational reasons. Will all checked in passengers please report at the check-in counter to collect their baggage. Nigerian Airways regrets any inconvenience to the passengers.'

It took Rose five minutes to take in the announcement. She waited for the other passengers to react. Someone next to her asked her not to panic. 'Meaning what?' she asked. Why didn't I pay that tout twenty naira. I would have been with Dora by now, she thought. Then the man who asked her not to panic came back and asked her whether she would like to go to the International Airport and take the flight going to London via Port Harcourt. 'No, I think I should go back home and try tomorrow morning,' she said without hesitation.

'Where is home?' the man asked.

'Oh, Ikoyi,' Rose said.

'Don't you think it is too late to travel to Ikoyi in a taxi?' the man said.

'Of course, yes. But my friend will have gone back to Aba by now. I will have nowhere to say in Port Harcourt.'

'If you don't mind, I can take you to Aba to your friend. A car will be waiting for me at the Port Harcourt Airport.'

'That's kind of you, thank you, but . . .'

'Wish you luck. I must go now,' said the man.

'I'll come with you,' said Rose.

They arrived in Port Harcourt after midnight. A company car was waiting and the driver drove them to Aba. 'The driver will drop me first since you are going into town, then he will take the car to his home in the village for it is too late for him to go home otherwise.' Rose thanked him profusely. At half past one in the morning, she found herself knocking at Dora's gate. It took the night watchman nearly three minutes to get up, and another two minutes to open the gate. He asked no questions. He shut the gate again and went back to sleep. Nightwatchmen in Nigeria are just there these days as part of the outfit of the house.

Dora hadn't gone to sleep. The lights were on, and so the door was open before Rose knocked. She thanked the driver and gave him a tip of ten naira. Dora embraced Rose. 'I was at the airport until eleven o'clock. Someone asked me to wait for the International flight but I didn't think you would think of taking it. Not many people, especially if they live in Lagos, know that they can take that flight to Port Harcourt. And of course, where does one go to from the Airport if one is just visiting at that ungodly hour? Welcome to Aba.'

Rose looked round her. Dora owned a beautiful seven bedroom house, tastefully furnished. The housekeeper and cook were still waiting. She got Rose something to drink while Dora showed her her room. No, she did not want to eat anything, it was too late. 'Have an apple then,' said Dora, 'I know you are keen on your figure.'

'They sell them here as well at four for five naira?' asked Rose.

'Yes, four for five naira. Don't tell me that they cost fifty pence for four in London. I love apples and I don't mind how much I pay for them,' said Dora.

In Rose's room Dora told her that her husband was leaving for home early the next morning and that was why he did not wait for her. He had said, 'I know you and Rose will keep awake like cockroaches all night, so see you when I return and say hello to Rose from me.'

'Has he changed much?' asked Rose.

'A good deal. But I have the whip hand. I am not a fool. Now my children have a father. That's all that matters.'

'And you, a husband?'

'Yes, and I a husband. But it is not the same. It can never be the same again Rose. What is left now is stark reality and commonsense.'

'Has he said anything about the German woman?'

'No, and I have not asked,' said Dora.

'Won't you ask?' Rosa was surprised.

'No, why should I? If he brings it up, all well and good. If he does not, it is his business.'

'Just like that?'

'Exactly like that. I didn't force him to return. He alone knows the reason for his return. As I said what is left now is

133

commonsense. I have built these businesses with my sweat and all the resources I could command. Should I have a brand new man to preside over them or my husband who is the father of my children no matter how badly he has treated me in the past, to preside over it? So there is nothing sentimental about having Chris back. I am facing reality. I am looking at my problem cold-bloodedly, and having arrived at my decision, every other consideration pales into insignificance.'

'In other words,' Rose said, 'love has nothing to do with it.'

'What is love, Rose? We loved when we were in school. After school days, one is not influenced in one's action by love, but by commonsense and convenience. Tunde understood. He too has a problem with the memory of his wife.'

'I should meet Tunde,' said Rose.

'You should.'

'What is he like in bed?' They roared with laughter. 'That I will not tell you. You have find out yourself. Tomorrow you will meet Tunde. Look, both of you can make a good pair. Interesting I had not thought about it before now. Rose you will like him, you wait and see, and when you like him, you will know what he is like in bed.'

'I have not come to Aba to hunt for husbands,' protested Rose. But her interest was aroused.

'Of course not, but you never can tell. Wait until you meet Tunde.'

Dora was up and doing by five in the morning. She supervised Chris' breakfast and he left for Onitsha before seven.

Rose was restless. Today was the tomorrow they talked about last night. She was like a child who was so excited about going to a party 'tomorrow' that she kept asking her mother whether today was tomorrow.

However at four Rose had a bath and got ready to meet Tunde. She wore a simple dress and no make up. At five Tunde drove in, and Rose came down. Dora came out of the

134

kitchen and introduced Rose to Tunde. Both Tunde and Rose opened their eyes and mouth in recognition. Dora looked on rather confused. 'We travelled together last night,' they both said.

'Isn't it a small world?' Tunde said as he gripped Rose's outstretched hand in greeting.

'And you did not know you had a mutual friend in Aba,' said Dora.

'The coincidence is amazing. And it was you who persuaded me to take the International flight to Port Harcourt,' said Rose.

'And you were hesitant, and when I said goodbye, you promptly decided to go with me. Amazing,' added Tunde.

'Please sit down, Tunde,' said Dora as she went to the kitchen.

'Don't you think the Nigerian Airways could be improved?' asked Rose.

'I am sorry . . . Oh can I call you Rose?'

'Please do.'

'I don't discuss Nigerian Airways or NEPA or P and T or bribery and corruption in Nigeria. It is a waste of time. If the Government wants these institutions to run better, all they should do is adopt the United States method. Which is, have them privately owned. Throw the door open to other air lines to compete with Nigerian Airways. Run the Nigerian Airways as a business which is what it is, and all will be well. Governments should leave those to the private sector. There is no business owned by any state government or Federal that runs at a profit.

'Try booking accommodation in the Presidential Hotel, Port Harcourt and you will be told that all rooms are booked. Then every year, the Government gives subvention to the Hotel. Half of the time, government functionaries use the hotel, and of course government pays, and no proper account is kept.

'You probably are right. I have not worked in the civil service.'

135

'Oh, I did for three years. I could stand it for only three years and left. I could not bear the waste of human resources, waste of money, waste of government property. A civil servant would without any qualms of conscience allow his government to loan let's say one thousand naira in his bid to recover his own one hundred naira. All the state governments and the Federal can manage quite well with just thirty percent of the staff they have, and be more efficient. Many public servants get paid for doing nothing.'

'In that case, you endorse what the present regime is doing in retiring civil and public servants,' asked Rose.

'Yes and no. The military cannot do what they are doing without harming a lot of people. Only a civilian regime can, given the singleness of purpose, and a genuine concern for the interest of the entire nation. Practically all public and civil servants have divided loyalty. He is either loyal to his tribe, his state or his religion or his friends but rarely his country.'

'You think this is due to our colonial heritage?' asked Rose, and Dora came in with a tray containing a well chilled champagne in an ice-bucket, champagne glasses and fried meat. 'I heard you, Rose,' she said as she placed the tray on the centre table.

'I don't discuss the frustrations in our country. I am practical and I am a market woman. You hear someone cataloguing all our woes as if he is an angel; that butter will not melt in his mouth. Then you are shocked to hear what that someone does in his own establishment. Tunde, please open the "sparkling wine" for us.'

With a practised hand, Tunde opened the bottle of champagne, poured into three glasses and toasted Rose's health. 'Welcome to Aba,' he said and they drank. 'Very well chilled,' he said.

'Dora is a wonderful hostess,' said Rose.

'Does that imply that you are not?' he said.

'Try her,' Dora said and they laughed.

While they were having dinner, Tunde invited Rose and

136

Dora to his home. But Dora declined, and she persuaded Rose to go. 'If you want to make it a dinner for just two its all right by me. But I would have loved to see you with your friend.'

Dora did not want to go. She had had a clean break with Tunde. What she was doing now was for her friend. Tunde had understood when she told him that she had to go back to her husband. And that she did not believe in extra marital activities. So it was. But they were still friends. He did things for her when she asked him and that was that.

At Tunde's home, Beethoven's sixth symphony was playing when Rose walked in. Tunde was in shirt sleeves and a white pair of trousers. He received her well and asked her to sit down while he got a glass of white wine for her. 'It was naughty of your friend not to have come. Of course I understand, but she should have accompanied you. However, I shouldn't grumble really. I respect Dora very much, and I am impressed by her magnaminity. Very few women will do what she has done.'

'Many will, Tunde. We women are different from men in many ways.'

'If you say so, my . . .' He stopped. 'You like classical music?' he asked instead.

'Not much. I appreciate it. They improve one's quality of life. But I am not fanatical about it, if you know what I mean.'

'I know what you mean,' Tunde said and laughed. 'Come, the food is ready.'

The food was superb. Grilled steak with onions, vegetables, potatoes and salad. Even salad. Tunde was not a Nigerian male. Nigerian males say salad is goat's food.

They ate and talked. Rose noticed that he had no servant, and said so. 'Well, I live alone here. My children are in the States. I don't really need a servant. I do my own shopping, wash my clothes and iron them. Once or twice a week, I hoover the floor. A servant will mess up this place.'

'How right you are. Your cooking is good. Who taught

137

you how to cook?' Tunde hesitated, and smiled sadly then said, 'My late wife whom I killed in a ghastly motor accident taught me how to cook. She . . .' He choked. 'Care for more vegetables?'

'Yes please.'

Nothing was the same after that. They were silent, but the silence was deafening. Dora rightly said that Rose and Tunde had a lot in common. Yes they did, but Dora saw only Tunde's sophistication and his taste. She did not see the aloofness and guilt. Tunde was a man searching for something he knew he had lost for ever. Rose could share with him his type of music, his books and even his solitude, but the memory of his wife and his guilt over her death, she could not share.

There were no photographs in Tunde's sitting room to record the past. All was tucked up in his memory. No one could break through. 'My wife taught me how to cook.' Those words destroyed everything. The food no longer tasted good in Rose's mouth. They could no longer talk freely. The ease with which they had conversed at Dora's house was gone. Rose longed for Dora's presence. If Dora were with her, it would have been different. But she was not there. Rose was on her own as always. Since leaving school, she has always been on her own. Ernest was beyond her reach, in jail or in protective custody, she did not know. Mark duped her and deserted her. Dora has come to terms with Chris and has her children; Agnes lost her lover but she has her husband and children; Olu always went back to his wife after each affair; Chinwe and Zizi had their youth to show. Even Tunde cherished a dear dead wife. But Rose, what had she?